A FLIP OF THE COIN

THE SELA HELSDATTER SAGA
BOOK ONE

RORI BLEU

ROSIE CHAPEL

First printing: 2023
ISBN: 978-0-6457084-5-5 (eBook)
ISBN: 978-0-6457084-4-8 (Paperback)

Ulfire Pty. Ltd.
P.O. Box 1481
South Perth
WA 6951
Australia

Cover Design: R Norman
Cover Image: Canva/Deposit Photos
Designed in Canva
Internal images: Canva/Deposit Photos.
Created using appropriate licences.

 Created with Vellum

A Note from Rori

This story, originally published in 2016, was my first attempt at a complete novel.

Recently, I decided it warranted a makeover and bullied... sorry, sweet-talked... my sometime co-writer, Rosie Chapel, into sharing the fun. Between us, we have revised the whole series, giving each book the loving edits, they deserve.

If you have been tempted into re-reading this book, dare I suggest revisiting all three of Sela's saga to see how time, experience, and the incredible patience of a skilled author/editor can make a story more readable.
If this series is new to you, I won't waste anymore of your time with additional platitudes.

Enjoy!

A NOTE FROM ROSIE

It is becoming increasingly clear that Rori Bleu is hell-bent on catapulting me out of my comfort zone at every opportunity. Not satisfied with pitching me headlong into wartime adventures, dystopian dramas, and vengeance novels... this time it's Norse sagas — *clutches head*.

I confess, when asked to help overhaul this series, I was hesitant because, while I love Viking history, I wasn't sure I was game to get involved in revising one, especially given my co-author's incredible talent. What on earth could I bring to the table?

I am endlessly glad I was persuaded. The journey through this trilogy has been an absolute joy, and I am honoured to have contributed even a small part to it.

Thank you, Rori!

A FLIP OF THE COIN

The Sela Helsdatter Saga

Book One

Rori Bleu

Rosie Chapel

PROLOGUE

Once Upon A Time...

Isn't that the way all happy stories are supposed to begin?

Once upon a time, there was a woman from the northern hinterlands named Sela.

Born of humble origins, through guile and mettle, she rose to be a formidable queen.

Those who pledged allegiance to Sela reaped rewards beyond their wildest dreams.

Against foes who dared threaten the reign and kingdom of their fearless shield maiden, these same men were willing to march into the jaws of death to defend her.

Sela's dominion grew beyond her fanciful imagination as, time and again, she marshaled her small band of warriors into battle against a superior enemy.

Where a less fanatical army would have suffered crushing defeat at the hands of barbarian hordes, her men plowed through these tribal opponents, ruthlessly, claiming land and treasure in Sela's name.

It was as though the gods marched among her soldiers, prepared to sacrifice themselves for her as well.

And that's where the happy story ends.

As with all warriors, the day of the queen's final battle arrived.

It marked the end of everything she held precious.

She had ignored the runes, which clearly foretold her impending doom.

Instead, she fell prey to the myths of her legendary prowess and to the words of her advisers, who assured her that, once more, the day would be theirs.

The battle was savage and bloody. Wave upon wave of invaders had stormed the field, while the queen's forces dwindled before her eyes.

The last sight she remembered of the day was of Peer, her most trusted adviser and consort, vanishing within the fray.

The sickening, violent pain of her skull smashing against a rock when she was dragged from her mount, ended the battle and her reign.

· · ·

After that, only fragments of memories remained.

Glimpses of chains, dungeons, and the blood-stained executioner's block were all she could summon up.

The one image, which would forever elude her, was of being welcomed to the Halls of Valhalla, to the Feast of Odin.

ONE

Sela awoke to a black maw of blankness which hung above her.

No matter how hard she tried to glean even a single flicker of a star, none were to be seen.

There was no horizon.

Her only visible landmark was an endless road, which originated out of nothing, became clearer as it bypassed her rock, then disappeared again.

With supreme effort, she managed to look at her body. She was stripped of any covering — save the chains which bound her to the rock and stretched her arms and legs taut, leaving her spread-eagled.

Even through the endless torture Sela was about to suffer, the heavy iron links would maintain their integrity with no sign of weakening.

Originally, she had believed her doom was to be a sacrifice to the deity of the warrior clan who had conquered her.

When she discovered, all too painfully, why she was here and for what perverse purpose — *that* fate would have been preferable.

One by one, they began to shuffle past her. The shapes, tangled and hideous, traveled down the road in a ponderous procession.

Their destination — Sela had no doubt — the Ninth World of Hel... Niflheim.

Her people believed it to be a cold, dark, dank, and misty realm, retribution for the evil which once prowled the fields of the world.

The way she was abused only strengthened her belief.

Sometimes, she saw a mere handful.
Sometimes, she lay alone and useless for an eternity.
Sometimes, they wandered along in their thousands.
Most continued on their way oblivious of her, but not all...

There were those who stopped and climbed upon the rock to debauch her. Creatures so twisted in pain and anger, they were beyond a sane description.

Her nostrils filled with the stench of their pure evil. The sickening scent of decaying flesh mingled with the vile odor of urine and faeces. Her stomach roiled in disgust. Her soft, pale skin was drenched and stained with blood and bile as they straddled her, one after the other.

They treated her as little more than a respite along the dark, lonely road, defiling her body, opening her with the same sickening pain as the day she lost her maidenhood to the marauders who had laid waste to her village when she was just a teen.

What wicked malediction caused her to be virginal with each new mounting?

As much as she willed herself to stare into the desolation beyond the vile parade, this was Hell. As much as she screamed for them to stop, to free her; inevitably, the corruption of Hell impelled her to succumb to the punishing violation of her body.

Sela became the very definition of the village whore; a designation she despised. Time and again, her body betrayed itself, delivering her to the lecherous lust these Hellish demons demanded. Her pleas to be saved became little more than a guttural petition for more.

Just when her body hovered on the pinnacle of ecstasy, the succubus spent itself and moved back into line. Her screams of anguish and despair seemed to spur the masses along.

Only after the last of those creatures finally disappeared into the void which devoured the road, did the darkness unleash itself, sending torrents of icy water to bathe her battered body.

The fires of her sexually charged frustration grew to welcome this quenching finale, though she knew it would never last.

This had been Sela's existence since that day.

How many eternities ago? her mind queried with numbed frequency. *Or was it this morning?*

Who could tell?

She lay on the stone pondering the reasons behind her exile to this forsaken road and when or if the gods might see fit to release her.

Sela doubted her freedom would be granted, or that a solution to this unending misery might be forthcoming.

Nonetheless, it provided a way to pass her existence until the dust on the road was kicked up once more.

Whatever represented time in the darkness, was also the breeder of immeasurable fear. The silence stretched out until Sela longed for company, even that of the fetid masses.

She strained her eyes attempting to scan the distance for any hint of their return.

That was when she noticed the gray desolation apparently bending into the shape of a single form.

At first, the identity of the enormous apparition remained elusive, her gaze captured by the rhythmic, glowing flutter which danced in front of it.

As its steps trod the road, at a measured pace, the shape coalesced into a man and the glint of flickering light, she had become fascinated with, revealed itself.

Shards of ice snaked through her and, although desperate to look away, appalled recognition froze her in place.

It was a coin.

Nay, not just any coin, it was *the* coin.

The coin she had found in the wreckage of her village when, eventually, she escaped her captors — who, once drunk, grew tired of abusing her.

The coin she had kept in her possession as a constant reminder that no man would ever have control of her again.

The same coin she had used to buy her kingdom.

She knew the current owner of the coin.

For the hand, tossing it so nonchalantly, was the one familiar with every curve of her body, able to reduce her to a quivering heap with a single touch.

Even now, what light the darkness gifted her, seemed to draw about him.

No, Sela corrected herself silently, *the illusion cannot be him.*

But it was... it was *Peer*.

Here was the man who had not only helped plan her conquests in battle, but also conquered her in the private confines of her chambers.

The man who had promised to give her a kingdom and riches beyond the realms of anything she desired... asking Sela for a single thing in return... her greatest treasure.

Her coin.

A battered, hand-forged piece of burnished gold, bearing a simple design. Three feet running in a perpetual circle — no beginning or end.

She remembered studying the coin when she found it, the imprint foreign to her and, to this day... night... whenever... she was clueless as to how it had journeyed into her lands.

Sela had allowed it to define her very life and soul.

Yet, she never thought of refusing Peer's request, which appeared as genuine as his pledge to stay by her side. He had held to his bargain, time and again, proving he was true to his name.

Peer was her lover. Her rock.

The irony of reality broadsided Sela. He had *never* intended to be *her* rock. From the outset, Peer's goal had been to lead her to *this* forsaken rock. He had played her for a fool right to the moment of her abandonment and capture. Anger welled within her.

Even as she willed herself to despise him, to lash out and wreak her vengeance, she longed to touch him, to have him touch her... like he used to.

For a moment, Sela was mesmerized by his obsidian eyes, then tore her gaze from his, knowing, if she did not, she would never be able to.

She screamed at him in a dialect she had not used since finding herself bound and helpless.

"Peer, as your queen I demand…"

Sela's blood ran cold at Peer's scornful bark of laughter, and the rest of her edict stuck in her throat. The black orbs of what she once considered the most beautiful and enchanting eyes she had ever beheld, now skewered her, to the depths of her soul.

"*Free* you, my Queen? Who are you to give *me* orders? Do you think you ever held dominance over me?" Peer taunted. "Come now, Sela, do not persist in disappointing me and, for the sake of the tired, old deity you believed in, stop using that barbaric tongue. You have no idea how maddening it is to listen to."

No sooner had Peer finished his admonishment than he waved his hand in her general direction, extorting a strangled cough to spill from Sela's mouth.

Satisfied his spell had taken hold, his attention left his prey and wandered down the road, observing it vanishing into the darkness.

"Not even worthy of Hell, itself," Peer chided absently. "Your existence was such a reckless waste of potential."

"Why…" Sela started, then stopped, startled to realize she was speaking in a language she had never uttered before, yet knew it as though it was her native tongue.

While intrigued at this strange development, knowing what magic he had inflicted upon her could wait. Right at this moment, his answer to the question uppermost in her mind was more important.

"Why would you do this to me? I loved you… I trusted you…" Sela's words trailed off as tears stung her eyes. She averted her gaze, refusing to give Peer the pleasure of seeing her sorrow.

Paying no heed to her misery, he sniped callously, "Love? The true interpretation is too powerful for mere mortals to comprehend.

"Your kind paint masterpieces honoring it, sing interminable operas extolling its virtues, and produce flowery line upon line of verse trying to capture its essence.

"In the end, you all are willing to declare your devotion to your fellow man in order to stab him in the back just to get that next piece of gold.

"Love? *Bah!*"

His fingers curled around her chin, impelling her to make eye contact.

The handsome features, she had once thanked the gods for gifting Peer with, were now distorted in contempt. "As for trust, you should be thanking me instead of weeping like a child. I gave you exactly what you desired — *immortality.*"

Peer paused to allow the weight of that single word to crush Sela's soul. With a pleased smile, he continued, "Why even now, children sing of you."

The dark chasm echoed with youthful voices. To Sela, it sounded like a choir of every child ever born. The mocking chorus filled her ears.

See the Queen all dressed in red.
See the axe fall on her head.
To stare will fill your heart with dread.
Dance instead for she is dead.

Peer chuckled. "No one remembers who you are or what you did, but the story of the cursed queen will be recounted forever. While this may not be the immortality you dreamed of, like a cheap gift, it's the thought that counts?"

He flipped her coin once again.

"Take your keepsake, for instance. This worthless, shiny trinket you gave me.

"It holds no value to anyone else except *you*. You gambled your entire existence on this single coin, but were willing to relinquish it in order to obtain..."

Peer glanced around.

"...to obtain what, my dear Sela? This? Do not pin your blame on me. This is a hell of your own design. In truth, it disturbs even me. Brava."

He marveled at how long it had taken Sela to recognize the architect of this place of misery.

It was **her**.

It represented the utter emptiness of her existence.

She had cared for nothing except her power, and her obsession for revenge, allowing her soul to darken, becoming as black as the maw.

Ashamed, Sela wrenched her gaze from his.

"Fear not, my Queen, for we are going to let the coin decide your destiny once and for all. Heads, you reside here until time itself ends. Tails, you gain your freedom by doing one small task."

"The price for your release is the soul of an innocent to replace you on the stone." Peer's fingers tiptoed up Sela's inner thigh, coming to a halt just shy of *Venus's honeypot* and, as was his habit, chortled like a schoolboy at the terms prudish humans in the sixteenth century used to describe what nestled at the apex of women's legs.

"Most of the miserable souls who ended up here, did so because of their weakness for that *sacred mound of woman-hood,* or as I like to call it, the True Gates of Hell. What kind of host would I be to deny them one last bit of flesh?"

"Sweet Odin's Mercy," Sela cried. "How could you make

such a demand? How can *I* condemn another poor soul to this punishment? Not even your depravity could imagine I would ever do such a thing."

"Oh, come now, dear queen. It's not such a difficult task and you know in your heart of hearts, you're already considering it," he replied, tossing the coin up and down on his palm.

TWO

Before Sela could open her mouth to protest, Peer flipped the coin.

Transfixed, Sela watched as it spun high in the air, an energy welled inside the metal causing it glitter as it fluttered into the darkness and vanished from sight.

She felt as though an eon had slipped by, while her fate hung in the balance, wondering whether the coin would return from the void.

A soft sigh escaped her when she saw Peer snatch it into the palm of his hand.

"Oh look, my dear. Tails. Fortune has favored you today."

Peer's sarcasm was not lost on Sela.

"The task I have in mind is child's play. I have no doubt you could be free in no time." He flashed a sickening smile.

"Though, from where you lie, who knows how long that could be?"

"Stop with the riddles, Peer, and tell me what you want."

"You have done a sterling job creating this place," Peer

admitted, admiring the bleak expanse. "It would be a shame to let it evaporate, but a deal's a deal.

"What is the cost of a stranger's soul compared with yours? I can see it in your eyes. You never could hide anything from me. Besides, you have already led more souls here at the end of your blade than you can count."

"Any I slew in battle died with honor," Sela objected hotly. "They fought for what they believed was right in their eyes. Surely, they at this very moment, feast with the gods."

"Sela, Sela, Sela... you still know how to amuse me. To whom did you suppose those souls traveling this road belonged? They were the ones *you* took... excuse me... *sent* to meet your gods, my sweet Instrument of Death. They were damned to never find rest, save the pleasures of this rock, for allowing greed — their true god, and the reason they drew swords — to devour them."

Peer scanned the road. Pausing his torment of the humiliated queen, he gripped her jaw, obliging Sela to follow his gaze.

"Are you aware of what lies at the end of the horizon? The return of this path. You already knew that though, didn't you?"

Silence descended as Peer gave her a moment to recall the lives she had taken. Although most died as she defended her kingdom, other lives were squandered expanding it.

Sela broke the hush. "If I do this, if I sacrifice another, what will become of me?"

"You, dear Sela, shall garner the riches you sought so desperately during your miserable existence. You will command my legions as my scythe of destruction, accountable to me and me alone. You shall dine on the flesh of those you vanquish, but never again feel the sting of mortal death.”

While Peer waxed lyrical about the glories awaiting Sela if she pledged herself to him, her eyes did not waver from the fluttering coin. It appeared to grow brighter with every flip, with each exaggerated promise which dripped from his tongue.

Sela was under no illusion that whatever Peer avowed would never be fulfilled and, if she succumbed to him, she was doomed to eternal perdition with no hope of salvation.

Unwittingly, Peer had just provided her with a vital piece of information. Apparently, all creatures, even the demons of Hell, had their weaknesses.

In Peer’s case, it was his monumental ego. His unerring belief, he already knew the option, Sela would choose even before she did, and that he could control her with sex.

Sela was not about to let that grain of knowledge go unused.

“What say you, woman? Damned to be defiled by the cursed, or immortality?

“You must enunciate your choice. Yes, yes, I agree,” giving her no chance to reply, “it is ridiculous, but we have regulations which must be followed. Bet you never imag-ined that Hell is run by a bunch of feckless bureaucrats,” Peer scoffed.

In the most submissive voice she could muster, Sela beseeched, “Peer, unbind me from this stone so, I may kneel before your might, and laud you as I answer.”

The words tasted rancid but she needed him to trust her. If this place *was* of her own making, Sela was about to teach Peer, she too controlled what was truth and what was a lie.

Peer paused the coin flip to consider her suggestion.

Stroking his chin, he studied her naked body. The fires of victory ignited in the vacant cavities of his eyes.

"Given any attempt to escape is futile, and that it has been an age since I entertained myself with that unquenchable libido of yours, your exhortation has merit. It will be music to my ears to hear you scream your adulation." Peer all but preened.

The shackles which had become one with Sela's wrists and ankles broke free. Slowly, she slithered from the stone onto her knees, frowning at the scarred flesh where the chains had been. Gingerly, she touched her wrist, unable to prevent a yelp of pain.

Peer shrugged off her agony with a cursory comment about the marks adding to her battle scars.

"Now I believe you were about to thank me for your freedom."

His fingers snarled through her hair, to pull her face towards his crotch.

Sela wanted to cry out as the gravel from that cursed road tore into her knees, but refused to give him the satisfaction.

Focusing all her fury and hatred for Peer, she concentrated on making him believe she wanted to serve him. This was Niflheim was it not? How could a demon such as Peer, in all reality, be able to discern the difference between the truth and a lie?

She drew in a breath, forcing herself to remember a time when she craved his flesh. She conjured a picture in her mind of when his scent ignited an animalistic desire, instead of the noxious aroma of putrefaction which now greeted her. If she ever had any chance of escape, she had to go through with her plan.

Even if she was successful, what then?

Slowly... oh so slowly... her hands crept seductively under his tunic to unfasten his belt. His breeches... made from a heavy and rather garish silk, she noted disdainfully, slid down his muscular legs.

Peer's manhood throbbed. Aye, she knew this bastard well. His excitement about what was to happen, his eternal conquest and domination of her, was consuming him.

Sela stifled a laugh when his body grew rigid as her fingertips and her lips drew him to the brink. Repulsed by the taste of his flesh, and the acidic droplets trickling onto her tongue, she persevered.

Setting a steady rhythm along his shaft, she glanced up when his fingers tightened in her hair, his hips grinding against her with each thrust.

Any time now.

Subtly, she urged his body around, taking care neither to change her tempo nor allow him to reach the point where his vile juices would fill her mouth. Sela willed herself not to beg for Odin's help. She could not fail in her mission.

From the corner of her eye, Sela spotted the massive boulder. Guiding Peer closer to it, she readied herself.

With an abrupt lunge, she drove him backwards against the rock. Peer let out a surprised howl as he landed, glowering at her in anger.

Sela did not stop pleasuring him. Engulfing him in her mouth, she swirled her tongue around his erection.

Secure in his omnipotence, he shrugged carelessly.

Sensing Peer's compliance, she lifted her gaze. Smiling wickedly, she released his engorged length with a playful *pop* of her lips.

Sliding up his tunic to reveal his taut body, she kissed her way from his hips to his chest; shimmying over his pebbled flesh with feline grace. Using her damnable punishment to her advantage, she gyrated wantonly against his bulging erection and, with the promise of full penetration hovering, leaned forwards to grasp his hands.

In the blink of an eye, she slammed Peer's wrists into the waiting shackles. The bite of the ancient iron wrested an agonized bellow and, involuntarily, his hands opened.

Sela watched the glittering coin drop from his grip.

"You, fen-sucked bitch," Peer snarled, "Release me at once or I will see your body never knows rest. I swear you will be used like the worthless whore you are for eternity.

"You may think you know suffering. I can assure you, what you experienced so far, will seem like a delicious daydream."

Sela snatched the coin from where it had come to rest on the road.

She could hear the stress of the chains trying to restrain Peer, threatening to shatter.

Ignoring his rant, Sela faced him.

Triumphantly, she brandished her cherished coin... *her very soul*, and, in her ancient tongue proclaimed, defiantly, "This should cover the cost to Valhalla."

She drew the coin back into the palm of her hand squeezing it tightly, confused by Peer's facetious laughter.

"Ignorant girl. You believe *that* will grant you safe passage to Valhalla? Did you really think a worthless coin possesses the power to free you from here?

"This is *Hell*. You go nowhere unless I say so."

Fear gripped Sela when the explosive crack of the first chain shearing, reverberated throughout the darkness.

Closing her eyes, she clenched the coin, which seared her flesh.

"Go ahead, you stupid wench, open your hand and gaze

at that miserable piece of trash. See what it has bought you."

Doing as he bade, Sela's jaw dropped when she saw the last traces of the coin burn into her palm, branding her with its mocking crest... and still she languished in Niflheim.

She heard the last chain sever and felt the blast of Peer's rage, as he prepared to direct his fury at her.

Strangely, a calm settled over her, like a cloak. Neither panic nor dread filled her. With an inner defiance, she confronted Peer.

"You may think you own this pit, but you don't. *I* do. I designed it and built it, and as such, I can destroy it."

Lifting her hand, Sela released a single strand of light from the coin's scar. The brilliance rent the merciless darkness. Its undiluted intensity compelled Peer to shield his eyes in pain.

"Stop Sela. You know not what you are doing. You will destroy us both."

Sela paid no heed.

The strand multiplied. As the illumination inundated the last of the void, it collapsed about Sela.

"Maybe so, Peer, but at least I'll celebrate knowing your death came at my hands."

Sela did not feel the explosion.
What she *did* feel was cold.

It wasn't the same cold she had suffered at the executioner's axe, claiming her life the first time.

It was more like a cold she had known as a child when she played with her siblings. It felt like — *could it be?* — the coldness of snow.

Cautiously, she opened her eyes to find herself curled in a mound of fresh snow. The sounds assaulting her ears were foreign and terrifying, causing her to wonder what Hell she had fallen into *this* time.

The chill overwhelmed her body, and she shivered uncontrollably.

"Damn you, Peer. Could you not have had the decency to clothe me?"

A voice filled the starlit night, "Had he done so, Sela, you would still be in Niflheim. Try this instead."

The warmth of something heavy materialized around her shoulders. Looking down, Sela noticed it appeared to be half-cloak, half-tunic.

Whoever thought about putting sleeves in a cloak? She nodded to herself, *clever indeed. It would make fighting in cold weather much easier.*

Pulling it close, Sela savored the snow, as well as being covered for the first time in centuries.

"Th-thank you, and where... I mean when... wha... this place?" Learning her fate, welcome or otherwise — and, given recent events, she suspected the latter — was imperative.

"It is called a coat, and welcome to New York, a city... which is an extremely large village... in a country called the United States of America. A land your people did not know existed. You have been absent from this world for some considerable time. It is the year twenty twelve."

There was a pause then, almost as an afterthought, the voice intoned, "The last month of which, for added interest, marks the cessation of the Mayan calendar, and signifies, for some, the end of the world. Rather blinkered but, perhaps, under the circumstances, fitting do you not think?"

Sela was momentarily distracted — *Twenty twelve? What in Odin's name does that mean? Mayan calendar? Who is this Mayan, and what is a calendar? Is it a new form of rune?*

She clutched her head, her mind spinning with the surfeit of information. "Calendar? Fitting? Why must you talk in riddles?"

With absolutely no clue to what the voice alluded, she opted to ask the one question, the answer to which she had some hope of understanding.

So, I am not in Valhalla?"

"No, little one, Peer did indeed tell you one truth. You have not earned your place in Valhalla just yet. There is much for which you must atone.

"Your penance is to locate Peer, who is somewhere in the vicinity, to destroy him, once and for all. Only then will you know peace. You have been given what you need to start your quest, Sela, but there are two things you must not forget.

"First, Peer is aware you are here, and has already set out to find you, for that is the only way he can return to Hell. Second, if you take the life of an innocent, you will forfeit any chance of freedom."

"Where do I start?" Sela entreated, to be met with silence.

"Hello? Are you still there?"

All she heard were the night sounds of this place called a city. A territory she knew nothing about and, within which, she had no clue what awaited.

Rising to her feet, Sela felt something hit her leg. Wedged in the pocket of the coat was a black metallic object which fitted in her hand perfectly.

As she withdrew it, her finger accidentally pressed a small lever at the bottom. She smothered a shocked squawk when a flaming projectile ejected and buried itself into a nearby tree. Fascinated, Sela watched the wood erupt in a shower of splinters.

"Well, now. That ought to come in handy."

As she returned the weapon to her pocket, her fingers brushed against something else secreted there.

It turned out to be a small case crafted of fine leather, inside of which was a card bearing her likeness. Peering at it, she saw, printed neatly, *Sela Helsdatter*.

"At least somebody has a sense of humor in all of this." Sela chuckled softly, sliding the card back from where it came.

Acknowledging, she had limited time in which to find Peer, Sela turned towards the bright glow of what the voice had called a city.

She wanted to thank Peer for teaching her the language she assumed belonged to this place and time... and then kill him.

THREE

Sela emerged from the depths of one forest, to discover she had already been consumed by another, only this one was made of stone.

So much stone, soaring above her to vanish into the leaden sky. While these towers looked sturdy, they were exceedingly tall. How did the Watch at the top, alert those waiting below?

She glanced back, and saw a marker which read Central Park. This confused her. Had not the voice called this place New York? She studied the stone forest again and gave a shudder nothing to do with the glacial air. This so-called city looked inhospitable.

Witnessing what had become of nature in this time made her want to weep, until a more pressing need demanded her attention.

While the magnanimous presence had seen fit to provide her with a coat, it seemed to have forgotten she was naked beneath it. Neither had it procured boots, and the snow was freezing her poor feet.

Now, more than ever, she was convinced it was none

other than Loki who was responsible for this. Sela vowed that, if and when, she chanced across that *bastarður* again, she would ensure he paid for his involvement.

The din which blasted her ears came as a shock after the peace of the forest, and she gaped in horrified fascination at the objects currently hurtling along a smooth gray track, presumably a road of this era, in front of her.

*What **are** these monsters?*

Enclosed carts of brightly colored, forged metal, mounted on four — what she surmised must be — wheels, but were like no wheel she had ever seen.

Where is the wood? Where are the horses?

They rolled along at a breakneck pace, and looked as though they would be extremely useful in a battle, although swinging an axe, or firing an arrow from the interior might be difficult.

In the midst of studying these strange wagons, Sela became aware she was losing all sensation in her feet. Glancing down, she noticed they were turning a concerning shade of blue. She needed to stop thinking and start moving.

Surely, somewhere in this city, there must be a leather worker who might be kind enough to give me a pair of boots. It looks big enough to require two or even three.

She peered across the gray road, its edges lit by torches in slender casings, but saw no sign of any workshops. She needed to venture deeper into the stone forest.

Dubiously, Sela watched the metal chariots whizz by; there was nothing for it, she had to cross the track. Holding her breath, she waited until she saw what looked like a gap and sprinted into the fray.

The objects swerved to avoid her. A cacophony of what sounded like battle horns blared from all sides, over which she heard furious commands to, "Get the hell out of the way."

One cart crunched into the rear end of another, which had screeched to a juddering halt so as not to hit Sela, who narrowly dodged being clipped by the yellow nose.

Sela sprinted to the opposite side, desperate to escape the cacophonous confusion. Panting from her headlong dash, she heard a man chastise, "Are you a freaking nutcase, woman?"

The man's irate question was accompanied by a hand gesture using only his middle finger. Assuming this was an appropriate way to greet people, Sela reciprocated in kind before disappearing down an alley.

She had not made it halfway, when she happened upon three figures in the darkness. Instinctively, Sela reached for her swords, only to remember her blades were no longer there to defend her against these *plágu, pests.*

The trio ringed Sela, like wolves circling for their kill.

The one she determined to be the leader of this band raked his eyes over her. Sela had never seen gold in anyone's mouth before, but this one must have struck the richest of all veins judging by the amount gleaming at her as his lips curled back in a lecherous sneer.

"Well, well, well, what we got here? Are you lost and in need of our help? Or do ya want to party?"

Sela's judicious step backwards took her into the arms of one of his cronies. She ground her teeth when she felt the swine slip his hand inside the coat.

As though he had never felt a woman's breast before, he blurted out, "Shit, she ain't got no clothes on."

The other two wrenched open Sela's coat, exposing her

body to the freezing night air. Her nipples were rock hard and stinging in the frigid wind.

"So, bitch, ya *have* come to party. I'm sure the three of us won't letcha down," Gold Mouth assured, mauling her breasts roughly with his dirty, calloused hands.

"I'd run, boys, while you still can," Sela warned ominously. "I don't have time to squander, playing with you three."

Gold Mouth backhanded her, bringing a trickle of blood to the corner of her lips. "Bitch, the only words I want to hear from your mouth are, *more please*."

Sela dabbed at the coppery flow with her tongue, her eyes never leaving his. Feigning regret, she whispered, "I tried."

Jerking her head back, Sela shattered the nose of the one holding her.

With a pained bellow, he released her, cupping trembling hands around the bloodied mess of his face.

Gold Mouth reached for his knife, only to fall to his knees when Sela's bare foot emasculated him with a ball crushing kick.

The third guy didn't wait around for his ass-whooping, choosing, wisely, to save himself.

Sela ignored him as he bolted, intent on disgorging a millennia worth of pain and torture on his two buddies.

Loki... the *presence* possessed all the hallmarks of the trickster god... may have forbidden her from killing innocents, but he *hadn't* said anything about beating them beyond recognition.

Satisfied she had discovered a legal loophole, Sela rammed her heel into Bearhug's face, making sure his nose would not heal properly, nor anytime soon.

The fragments of teeth he spat out, fueled Sela's zeal.

She stopped when she heard the Voice grousing in her ear, "What did I *just* say about taking unnecessary lives?"

"Allow me to correct you. You said not to *kill* innocents, but nothing about protect—"

"Stop twisting my words."

"You would be the one to know when somebody does, wouldn't you?" Sela retaliated.

Ignoring the tirade which followed, she paused long enough to listen to the gurgling bubbles of blood pouring from the wreckage of Bearhug's face, reassured he remained among the living.

In an aggrieved aside to the annoying deity, she contested, "I am playing by your rules."

Her ire not yet doused, Sela eyeballed Gold Mouth.

Seeing her advancing like a rabid dog, Gold Mouth scrambled for his knife, slashing it upwards to defend himself.

The blade glinted under the alley's single streetlight.

Sela hesitated, evading the thrust at her belly by a whisker, which deluded her assailant into believing he had regained a semblance of control.

"Come on, bitch. Come at me now." He jabbed the knife at her, accentuating his threat.

A smile quirked Sela's lips as she remembered the tree in the park. Pulling the gun from her coat pocket, Sela squeezed the trigger.

The fire kicked the magical projectile from the end of the barrel, severing two of Gold Mouth's fingers and cata-pulting the knife somewhere beyond his grasp.

Spinning the gun in her hand, she swung the grip hard at his temple, dropping him into an unconscious heap next to the bloodied mess of his companion.

Lavishing a precious moment to check she had not killed Gold Mouth accidentally, she beat a hasty retreat.

Emerging from the alley, she groused aloud, just in case Loki — absolutely certain he was the persona behind the Voice — was listening, "Odin's beard, you fool, the least you can do is tell me *who* you consider to be innocents."

As the fires of her adrenaline rush began to subside, the bite of the snow reminded Sela she still needed boots. Spying a large building, its windows aglow in candlelight, a faint glimmer of hope arose.

Perhaps it is an inn, Sela pondered, *and the keep might be swayed into providing shelter from the chill night in exchange for work.*

Sela hurried down the street, to be diverted by a size-able, silvery, solid-looking receptacle standing in front of the inn. One of the bright torches glimmered above it, illu-minating several bags of clothing scattered about the vessel, and hanging from its open shutter.

It struck her as odd that a trader would leave his merchandise spread about in such a haphazard way.

What if the same band who attacked her in the alley had struck here as well?

Alarmed, Sela pawed through the discarded wares in search of a body. Finding no trace of an injured merchant, she decided to rifle through the sacks of clothes for her own benefit.

"If the man is so neglectful of his wares that anyone can help themselves, surely it is not regarded as stealing when I do?"

The logic seemed sound to her and, if anyone happened by, they would understand as well. Without waiting for a rebuttal from Loki, Sela combed through the bags in earnest.

She snagged a peculiar garment by a strap and pulled it out to examine it. The strap was connected to two domed pieces resembling cups, a tassel was sown in the center of each.

Sela wondered whether it was a headscarf, although she had no idea as to the purpose of the tassels.

The material was strange to her touch. Instead of the wool and linen she was accustomed to, the piece was woven of a thin fabric, which she guessed was some sort of silk, and studded with beads and gems. *Not particularly useful in protecting a person from the chill of winter.*

Besides, she had possessed silk in her time. It had cost a small fortune and no one would waste such material for a frivolous piece of clothing. She tossed it aside.

The next item from the bag was a skirt, or at least Sela judged it to be. It was made of the same material as the strange scarf and matched in color. It possessed slightly more fabric than its mate, but not by much.

Sela held the skirt against the front of her coat, attempting to picture it on her.

It did not take long for her to discover the coat was too capacious to gauge the fit of the clothing, adequately. Doffing it, Sela draped the coat carefully over the shutter.

Free of encumbrance, she held the flimsy garment against her hips to compare its measurements, quickly deducing the silk would be little more than a band and definitely would not cover her rear.

As she studied the outfit more closely, a frown tugged at her lips.

"What manner of deviants populate this hellhole? Not even the slaves of my realm would have humiliated themselves with such a manner of dress," she muttered out loud.

With only the whistle of the zephyrs responding to her query, Sela offered the skirt to Njǫror, the Norse god of the winds. Watching it flutter away, she was sure the old deity would enjoy playing with it.

A sudden gust nipped her skin, encouraging her to check another bag.

The next one contained colorfully dyed tunics and pants which seemed more suited to a woman's body. The merchant had stitched the word *LEE* into the backs of the clothing which confused Sela. Was it the mark of the weaver, like those made by the stonemasons or blacksmiths of her day, or was it the crest of the owner.

"An odd crest if 'tis so. No image, just letters," Sela mused.

She gave up trying to comprehend the meaning of the tags and rummaged through for warmer clothing.

Her fingers ran across a thick tunic. She pulled it from the bag and shook it out. It appeared worn and dingy, but not threadbare.

Further foraging revealed a plethora of similar attire.

Her attention fixed on the treasure trove, Sela failed to notice a man approaching. Silently, he observed her lithe, naked form as she bent to examine each piece of clothing.

Much to his surprise, and delight, the woman exuded a remarkable confidence despite her nakedness.

He marveled at the way her alabaster flesh sparkled under the streetlight as the snowflakes clung to her and how the cold did not seem to bother her.

A twinge of shame crept through him for not averting

his gaze from her nudity, but it was a rare treat to be presented with such a beautiful creature.

He spoke softly so as not to spook her, "I'd recommend the jeans and sweatshirt, and the sooner the better before you freeze to death, my child."

Sela jumped at the sound of his voice.

Dropping the tunic, she scrabbled to retrieve the pistol from her coat, but cold fingers and panic do not mix. The heavy garment slipped from her grasp to crumple in a heap on the snow.

Ignoring it, Sela swiveled to face the intruder, leveling the weapon in his direction, one finger tightening around the trigger.

Pausing long enough to see whether Loki intended to intervene to prevent her from discharging the explosive fire, the sight of the man stepping into the arc of the torch light, his hands raised, did the trick instead.

"Don't shoot, please. I mean you no harm. Feel free to take whatever you want."

"I was not stealing," Sela defended herself. "I was merely inspecting the merchant's wares to purchase suitable clothing." The lie sounded terrible even to her.

"What merchant? And would you mind lowering the gun, or at least, let me put my arms down? I promise, I won't hurt you," the man reassured.

He didn't wait for her reply.

"With regards to you *shopping* from a merchant, you're stealing from my parish's donation bin, but who am I to argue with the armed, naked woman."

He sent her a lop-sided grin. "I guess we can discuss the legality of your actions once we get you out of the cold."

Stooping, he picked up her coat and the discarded bag.

He passed the coat to her free hand then walked to a nearby building.

"I hope you don't mind canned stew for dinner, they didn't teach culinary skills at seminary."

Sela shrugged into her coat, watching him trudge through the snow to the largest longhouse she had ever beheld.

This cannot be the home of any mere priest. Are they not required to pledge poverty?

The question igniting her concern was not the only cautionary sigil to scribe itself on Sela's brain.

There was one man brave enough to address her so casually. One from whom she thought she had escaped in a hellish blaze, only to be told he had survived.

The nagging voice, suspicious about the true identity of the man who was offering her shelter, was screaming for her to stop.

The frosty night denied her a sensible decision.

FOUR

Sela's eyes narrowed when the figure paused momentarily in the doorway, the outline of his body silhouetted in the warm glow spilling from the house.

He turned to motion her once more to follow him inside before vanishing from sight.

A thought slithered through her mind. *Loki, it cannot be this straightforward. You would not deliver Peer on so obvious a platter — would you?*

Shoving the weapon into her pocket, fingers firmly around the grip, she crept towards the longhouse, exercising a healthy dash of caution.

Stepping through the door, Sela hesitated. Uneasiness reared its ugly head at the religious trappings on the walls, which triggered memories of the first time she had encountered Peer.

She had found him unconscious on a beach after a particularly tumultuous storm.

"No doubt Ægir spat him up from the bowels of the sea after one of his parties," Sela had muttered.

His clothing was strange, resembling more warrior than priest, but bore the markings of the foreigners who had invaded her lands from the South, attempting to strip her people of their gods and replace them with their own.

She had considered killing him then and there, but the beauty of his face saved him.

Instead, she found herself dragging him back to her hovel to tend to his wounds and nurse him back to health.

The rest was just cruel history.

To this day, whenever it was, she cursed herself to Odin for not ridding the world of Peer when she had the chance.

Sela circled the room studying each of the icons adorning the walls.

While most were, in Sela's opinion, gloomy scenes of a mother and child, or a hearty meal attended by a group of men in long robes, or a dead body under a cross on a hill, or gilt edged and intricate lettering — one or two depicted a motif reminiscent of the Valknut, a tri-cornered symbol Sela associated with Odin.

Her nose crinkled in confusion. *In the centuries since her death, had the gods of different peoples formed an alliance?*

The priest interrupted Sela's train of thought. "If you're planning to add those to your shopping list, please refrain from doing so. I'm not sure I could explain to the bishop why they went missing, which would lead him to question why I had a woman here in the first place."

"I assure you, Priest," Sela retorted. "I have no intention of taking your precious art, or your precious clothing... so important, you left it strewn across the snow. I was merely contemplating how much to..."

"Yes, yes, you simply want to pay for the clothing you would have stolen, had I not happened by, and be on your way," the priest countered wearily. "I've heard it all before."

Changing the subject, he waved his hand to Sela's left, instructing her as he turned to leave the room. "You'll find the bag in the bathroom down the hall. Hurry up and get dressed. There's nothing worse than cold stew. I guarantee the longer it takes you, the colder it's going to get."

Sela squinted along the dim passageway in the general direction of his gesture.

There were a couple of doors to choose from but she had no idea which was the bathroom — or what a bathroom was for that matter.

The priest chuckled when she did not move, obviously in a quandary.

He clarified, "It's the second from the end. Please join me in the kitchen when you're ready."

Padding down the hall, she slipped through the door the priest had pointed out, amazed to find there was a candle, maybe several candles, burning in a clear, domed bowl suspended from the ceiling. *How did they make that?*

She would ponder the miracles of this age later. Lifting the bag onto a small stand, Sela removed the gray tunic, advising her to visit some Grand Canyon, and a pair of dark blue pants, the priest had called jeans.

Placing both on the vanity, Sela was in no hurry to dress. If the priest was going to gripe about a cold meal, that was his problem. Her attention was riveted on the ancient, claw-foot bathtub.

Yes, its appearance had altered in the thousand years since she had last indulged; but, by Odin's beard, she had not forgotten its use and was *not* going to miss out on this chance.

She studied the knobs fixed to the rim and toyed with them.

To her amazement, water gushed out of the shiny curved pipe between the knobs and, just as quickly, disappeared down the hole in the bottom of the tub.

Looking for something to plug the blasted outlet, she grabbed another tunic from the bag and stuffed it in as far as she could.

"Problem solved," she chirped, pleased with her ingenuity.

She fiddled with the knobs until the water was just shy of scalding. Sitting on the edge of the tub, Sela watched in childlike fascination as the steam rose from the surface.

The eons in Niflheim had dulled her ability to determine extremes of temperatures on her body, but the vapors triggered memories of the hot springs her family had washed in when she was a child.

Lost in thought, she did not register that the water was about to breach the confines of the tub.

With the level millimeters from disaster, she spun the knobs the opposite way. The cascade dwindled and stopped. She beamed at the taps — a clever contraption, much better than buckets.

Sela cocked an eye at the door. Her mistrust of the priest

had not abated, especially given her present vulnerability, and she placed the pistol within easy reach on the toilet seat... just in case he decided to walk in uninvited.

Satisfied with her protective measures, Sela climbed into the tub and, with a tired sigh, sank under the steaming water. Unaware of Archimedes' principle on the displacement of fluid, this catapulted a dense wave over the rim, soaking the bathroom floor.

Sela cared naught about the flood. A careless glance at the mess, produced nothing more than a disinterested humph. *It is the priest's longhouse. If it upsets him, he can clean it.*

Almost instantly, the heat transformed her pale flesh into a vivid red canvas. The brilliance of the color resembled the bloody masses who had paraded past her.

Relieved she was no longer enduring their torture, Sela could not prevent a morose laugh. All the same, while glad to note her body was receptive to this new life, Sela knew she did not belong in this era.

Her eyes drifted shut.

The other consequence of the water was not quite as welcoming.

Sleep had been an elusive pleasure to her in Niflheim. At any time, the herd could reappear, putting Sela on perpetual guard.

Here, in the safety of the tub, she felt at ease.

An error quickly recognized.

• • •

Her mind's eye perceived a field. The familiar, repellent odor of slaughter swamped her and, although Sela saw no trace of the dead, she sensed their proximity.

In striving to look away from the nightmare, she found herself roaming the plains, leaving utter devastation in her wake, until she arrived at the ruins of an immense longhouse.

Peering up, she tried to judge its height, but the sloping roof — calling to mind a ship's hull — vanished into a pallid sky.

She screamed, knowing where she was.

Sela commanded her body to wake, but the warmth of his breath against her ear weakened her resolve. Sela felt his arms wrap around her waist, the bulge of his cock nestled against her. She slackened in Peer's embrace.

One hand explored her body. Strong fingers cupped her breasts, tormented her nipples, threatening to ignite her passion, while the other melded her to him. Not even in her sleep was she safe from him.

Peer whispered, "It is not too late, my Queen. I can still give you everything you want. You have seen how hopeless this world has become. It begs for our rule. Even now your army is prepared to enter battle at your command. Victory is but a word from your lips, Sela."

A searing pain in her palm lodged the acknowledgment in her throat. Lifting her hand, she saw the charred scar of the coin ignite into a blinding flare.

Sela thrust her hand over her shoulder, finding and clutching Peer's cheek.

She felt him slump, and spun to see him fleeing across the barren expanse.

Issuing a challenge to the diminishing figure, "Face me in the flesh, vermin, so we can finish this once and for all."

The field vanished along with Peer. Fighting to open her eyes, Sela scrabbled for the pistol.

Fingers snagged her wrist, holding it firmly.

Sela appealed, "Peer, release me, release me."

To the surprise of her subconscious, it was not Peer who answered.

"Wake up, Sela. You're having a nightmare. Chri..." the priest caught himself before he blasphemed. Gathering his wits, he tried again. "You almost drowned."

Sela's eyes flew open to see the priest perched on the rim of the tub. Automatically, she reached for the gun, positive she knew the priest's true identity. Her hand flailed against the toilet lid, searching for it.

The priest cleared his throat, and held up the pistol. "Are you looking for this? Don't fret, I'll keep it safe until you settle down. I'm not sure who this Peer is, but it sounded like the two of you were having a hell of a fight and I don't want you to shoot me accidentally."

Sela hissed, "If you're not that demon spawn, how do you know my name, priest?"

The priest tossed her card into the tub. "New York IDs provide a surprisingly large amount of info on a person, Sela Helsdatter. We can talk more in the morning. I'm going to bed."

"Don't worry about your gun," he added, "even the Catholic Church has the forethought to provide a secure safe for our most revered relics."

Relaxing his grip on her wrist, he rose and pointed to a thickly knitted sheet hanging on a rail. "There's a clean towel for you. After you get dressed, you'll find your dinner in the kitchen and you can sleep on the couch tonight."

He paused at the door, fighting the urge to turn around. "There's a mop in the kitchen pantry, use it to clean up the mess. Oh, and allow me to introduce myself. My parishioners call me, Father Thomas."

Morning found Sela on the couch, watching the sunrise. A victim of Peer's treachery the last time she succumbed, she had fought against sleep, damned if she would suffer a repeat.

Even the forgiving glimmer of the dawn did not improve the city, in fact, it looked dirtier than it had the night before... if that was remotely possible.

The towering buildings, which lined the road as far as Sela could see, loomed over the ground beneath, as though hiding it from the sun.

Are these people afraid of the light?

She could not comprehend why anyone would want to construct such monstrosities, they left her feeling dead inside.

Where was the wild game in this land of stone? How did the people eat?

She had not seen a single set of tracks, not even in the snowy park, to indicate the presence of beasts, nothing save the odd dog scrounging for scraps, and they had no meat on their bones.

"Doubtless killed off by those rumbling horseless carts," she muttered balefully.

Discarded debris poked through the blanket of snow trying, unsuccessfully, to conceal it. Sela began to wonder whether she was still in Niflheim, for not even she could have conjured up such a bleak scene.

Mercifully, movement whipped her attention away from the window.

She looked up to see Thomas offering her a mug before he settled on the couch. Sela studied the steaming dark liquid. The aroma was tempting, but she was hesitant to drink anything he handed her.

Stalling, she greeted him with a cursory smile, "Good morning, Priest."

She watched him take a gulp of the brew.

That he did not clutch at his throat or foam at the mouth was not enough to induce her to risk a sip. Her drink could be the only one he poisoned.

Thomas set down his mug on the small table in front of them and reached for hers. Taking a large swallow, he handed it back to her. "I'm not sure what or who is to blame for your trust issues, Sela, but be assured, I'm not going to murder you.

"Though I *have* been told my coffee could exterminate cockroaches. And please, call me Thomas. You sound like you're swearing at me when you call me *Priest*."

"I'm sorry, Pri... I mean, Thomas. The last of your people I encountered did not leave a good impression," Sela murmured, and allowed herself to taste the beverage he called coffee.

The bitter bite of the fluid warmed her insides. She took a second gulp. Not even Odin himself could prevent her from draining this... this... *suttungmjaða* — a mythical beverage believed to transform even the most mind-numbing dullard into a silver-tongued scholar. *A fitting moniker for, surely, this ambrosia must be a gift from the Gods.*

Sela glanced at Thomas's mug, unattended on the table.

Without asking, she switched their cups, chuckling under her breath. "Your coffee is not that bad."

"Uh, thanks." Thomas picked up the empty mug. "Let's see what you think of my eggs."

He rose from the couch and headed for the kitchen.

Sela's stomach rumbled at the thought of fresh eggs.

Mistrust of the priest, combined with outright fear, had prompted her to leave the previous night's meal untouched. Her body decided now was the appropriate time to scold her for that mistake.

On silent feet, she followed Thomas, relishing the coffee.

Sela leaned against the kitchen door frame, watching Thomas scrape the congealed remnants into a barrel.

"I warned you about letting the stew go cold..."

More interested in observing him, than listening to him drone on about the evils of wasting food, especially this magical stew, Sela tuned him out.

Mid-monologue, he stooped to replace the lid onto the barrel, and his heavy robe sagged open enough to provide her with a pleasing glimpse of his muscular chest.

Nice. The priest obviously exercises. Sela grinned into the last of her coffee. *Wonder what else that robe is hiding?*

Unfortunately, the robe ordained it improper to supply an answer.

Registering what she hoped was the end of his lecture, Sela padded to one of the chairs tucked around the table. She didn't offer to help, the priest had everything in hand.

Thomas had other ideas.

"No, you don't. You steal from my donation bin, pull a gun on me, and trash my bathroom. Then, you dare to commit the most heinous of crimes by depriving me of my morning coffee. No, my dear woman, you will serve your penitence by assisting with breakfast."

Sela was about to object to his accusations, but Thomas did not give her the chance, and tossed an egg in her direction.

This caught her off guard, but she managed to snatch it mid-flight. Her quick reflexes surprised her as much as they did Thomas.

Thomas whistled in amazement. "Any more tricks up your sleeve?"

Sela studied the egg for a moment before she joined Thomas at the opposite side of the small island.

A fleeting memory of wielding one of her favorite swords with equal finesse, coaxed a faint smile to her lips. "Yeah, I'm a carnival freak. For my grand finale, I juggle knives and torches."

Thomas slid a bowl made of glass and the egg carton to her across the bench. "Kitchen's too small for that. How about cracking the rest of these and helping me to make scrambled eggs."

Agog at the trappings in this kitchen... *where was the fire pit?* Sela tried not to blurt out the string of questions clawing at her throat, hoping that by close scrutiny, the function of these shiny gadgets would become clear.

She was not about to tell this man, she had no idea how anything worked, he would think her demented.

It was one thing to be informed she was living twelve hundred years in the future, and quite another to adapt. *Thanks for nothing, Loki*, she griped inwardly.

At least she knew how to crack eggs and, taking care not

to break the finely crafted bowl, she did her best not to drop the shells into the mix and the pair made small talk while they prepared breakfast.

Sela listened to Thomas describe the financial hardships of the church and how the numbers of parishioners had been declining steadily during the past few years.

She knew he was talking for talking's sake while he tried to figure out how to encourage her to share her own story.

Given I cannot fathom it myself, how on earth can I explain it to this man of faith? He would probably stab me with one of those crosses if he discovered where I was before I appeared on his doorstep. Mind, Priests are supposed to believe in and understand Hell, aren't they?

No, she concluded, *he would never believe something like that. How could he? She had yet to accept it.*

Instead, she concentrated on something she found infinitely more palatable.

Thomas... whom, she surmised since he did *not* murder her in the night, probably was not Peer... stood a good *ell* taller than her, depending on whose arm was measuring. She examined his features more closely while he continued the mundane task of cooking.

His black hair complemented the deep hue of his skin. She placed him as being passed his thirtieth year, although the creases around his eyes told of a life harder than others of a similar age. His hands were strong, long fingers tapering to clean and neatly shaped fingernails.

Her rumination was interrupted when she spotted her own reflection in the back of a spoon.

Despite spending the last thousand years chained to a rock, she posited her appearance was as fair as most. Her eyes were the brilliant blue of her father, her hair — the fiery auburn of her mother.

She missed her parents deeply.

Sela was relieved to see she had been spared the ravages of war and eternal punishment, save the battle scars she wore as badges of honor.

For just a moment she studied the pale line which marred her jawline.

A childhood souvenir.

A consequence of challenging her brother to a wooden sword fight. The subsequent wound resulted not only in the scar, but also a severe scolding. To this day she could hear her mother's admonishment regarding the necessity of maintaining her beauty if she ever expected to win a husband.

"That boring am I?" Thomas asked, feigning affront. "If you're done admiring yourself in my spoon, would you care to join me?"

Dropping her gaze from the utensil, Sela hoped the priest did not notice the blush, his words had elicited. Scooping up the implements he had indicated... *what had he called them? cutlery...* she made herself comfortable at the table.

The inviting aroma of breakfast sparked a ravenous appetite in Sela.

Electing not to wait until the priest had finished thanking his deity for the food, Sela — ignoring his mildly indignant expression — dug into the bounty, devouring the scrambled eggs and bacon Thomas had served.

Secretly, Sela was impressed at how handy Thomas was in the kitchen... especially for a man.

The food also provided an acceptable cover for the awkward silence which descended. Thomas was content to let Sela eat. He did not relish the thought of seeing crumbs splatter from this beautiful woman's mouth, if he dared speak.

Oblivious, Sela savored her first food in more than a millennia and, for a while, the strange duo were occupied doing justice to their respective meals.

Her hunger satiated, Sela settled back in her chair. She ought to be embarrassed at her greed, but what did it matter?

She realized she was staring at the man across from her. Worse, she was taking mental notes about him... and wondering what it would be like to be bedded by an actual mortal instead of some corpse.

He is *pleasing to the eye.*

She stabbed at the last of her egg with her spoon, chasing it about her plate rather than eating it.

Her gaze returned to Thomas, who was in the midst of delivering a dissertation regarding the proper preparation of eggs.

Hmmm... you might be handy with a frying pan, Priest, but can you pleasure a woman with the same expertise? I have my doubts, and such a deficiency could explain why you chose to become a priest.

I'm definitely relegating you to the 'someone not to bother sleeping with' list.

"Don't you agree?"

Sela looked up to see Thomas studying her speculatively.

"Hmm... ah... yes... without hesitation you should."

Should? Should what? Sela's conscience mocked her.

Thomas gave her a queer look before carrying on with his lecture.

Glancing at her plate, she resumed her musings.

You are centuries younger than I, anyway, and a priest to boot — although from what I've seen so far — you're probably not a very good one.

As much as she hated thinking about him...

Peer was the antithesis of Thomas.

He *was a priest who could rally thousands into battle with an inspirational oration about serving justice.*

Sela reckoned the best Thomas could incite was mass desertion.

Swallowing a sigh, her thoughts strayed to what it had cost her to become involved with a priest in her prior life.

That certainly didn't end well.

Sela determined, her best recourse, once attired appropriately and her belly full, was to thank Thomas for his hospitality and be on her way.

Then he placed another mug of Odin's mead before her.

It threw out the best laid plans into one of the dirty snowbanks.

"*Bölva pér, Priest,*" she murmured. *Curse you.*

"Insulting me again, are you?" Thomas quipped. "If you think me dull, you should have said something."

"No, of course not. I found you fascinating. I was thanking you for pouring me another mug of this delicious brew." Sela tried to cover.

"Danish?" Thomas hazarded.

"Pardon?" Sela squirmed uneasily; she remembered and hated the Danes.

"I'da guessed Sweden, you know, with your cool accent and brilliant blue eyes, but that angry red hair just doesn't fit."

Sweden? Does he mean Svíþjóð? If he does, I would war against those lands just because he favored them.

Grimacing at his abhorrent observation, Sela bit her tongue, growling to herself, *how stupid can this priest be to insult a Norse Queen in such a flippant manner?*

On an indignant huff, she replied, "I am Norse."

"Norse? Don't you mean Norwegian?" Thomas was intrigued by her terminology.

Sela thought quickly. *Norwegian? Was that the modern term for Norðwegr?* For the sake of argument she would accept it. *By Odin, these people certainly knew how to mutilate a beautiful language.*

"Yes, I meant Norwegian. Well, my family is. They emigrated from a small village a couple of generations ago. My grandmother only spoke Norse, which is how I learned it."

"Interesting," Thomas observed as he rose to clear the table.

He pressed Sela for more details. "Do you have family? Ought you to contact them to let them know you're ok?"

Presuming this 'ok', he bandied about, meant unharmed, Sela chewed her lip, unsure how to respond to that question, or why the priest cared enough to ask. She supposed it was a part of his job to reconnect troubled people with their families, but all it did was make her feel more alone.

"No, I haven't seen them for a very long time," she replied, *and that is an understatement.* "I doubt I shall ever see them again."

"Sorry to hear that, Sela," Busy putting the dishes in the sink, Thomas did not turn around. "I come across a lot of similar situations. Things happen, wrong words are said. Sometimes its fixable, sometimes the break down is irreversible. I just try to pick up the pieces."

Sela seized the opportunity to swing the conversation away from her. "Tell me something, Thomas. Why are you a priest? I have run into men of your belief before, but am having a hard time picturing you in this role. Tact does not seem to be your strong suit."

Thomas laughed as he rejoined Sela at the table, "Nor is it yours. Ok, I'll tell you what, let's play a game. Question for question. I'll answer yours as long as you answer mine."

Sela smiled knowing most of what she was going to give the priest was a lie anyway. "You have my agreement, and that was your first question."

Thomas sipped his coffee in what Sela judged to be a stalling tactic rather than in simple enjoyment of the drink.

She was about to call him on it when he spoke.

"Sometimes, God waits for the darkest moments in a person's life to call him to serve." Thomas swallowed another mouthful of the rich brew.

Sela could see sorrow etched on his face.

"When I was growing up, my family life was anything but a television sitcom. Both of my parents drank... a lot. My father used me as a punching bag when he over-indulged. Told me it was to toughen me up, make me a man. That went on until I was about ten, when he decided he'd had enough of his family and disappeared.

"My mother blamed his desertion on me because I was a burden. I guess I was a burden for her, as well, because her drinking increased, and she took up where good old dad left off. At fourteen, I'd had enough, and ran away."

Sela covered Thomas's hand with hers. Compassion was an emotion she struggled with, but she managed a sincere, "You don't have to go on. I can see this is bringing up bad memories."

"No, it's ok. I'd definitely fall into your estimation of me as a priest if I can't open up about myself.

"I was homeless, doing what I had to do to survive. Learned how to drink like my old man by the time I was seventeen and discovered I had inherited his penchant for violence when I was drunk, which led to more fights than I can remember.

"I met a girl and we started dating. Kinda blows your concept of priestly celibacy, eh?" Thomas shrugged, and mustered up the semblance of a smile. "Eventually, we moved in together, but my drinking didn't stop, nor did the violence."

Thomas's voice dropped almost to a whisper, "One night, I put her in the hospital. Nearly killed her, truth be told. That's when I made a promise to God. If she survived, I'd turn my life around, but you can't bargain away your sins.

"She lived, but suffered permanent brain damage. Guess beating defenseless people was my superpower. Anyway, God kept her alive, so I held up my end of the deal and became a priest."

He paused to clear a throat suddenly clogged.

Back in control, he continued, "I still visit her a couple of times a week just to see how she's doing. She has no memory of me, just that I'm a friendly priest who stops by to say hello."

Sela wanted to console him for sharing something so painful, but that required letting him get close to her, something she could not afford.

She attempted to lighten the mood, "And where did you learn to make this horrible coffee?"

Thomas raised his hand. "First, it's not horrible, I can tell because you're on your umpteenth cup, and second, that's a question. You don't get to ask another one yet. It's my turn."

Sela knew the question even before he broached it, but dreaded it all the same. Had their roles been reversed, she would have asked it last night at the donation bin.

"So why did I find you naked..."

Sela interrupted, "I was not naked, I had a coat."

"Not when I saw you. And *no* interrupting. What's your story?"

It was Sela's turn to take a stiff drink, deciding, since Thomas had been so brutally honest with her, she should be courteous enough to return the gesture... to a point. Then she would leave it to him to decipher what was true.

She inhaled a steadying breath, then exhaled with resolve.

"Mine is not very different from most.

"Girl from a small village is enticed to follow a mysterious stranger bearing candy. Soon, girl's life is overflowing with shiny things which led her to do other things she's not proud of... but, by then, she did not care because she is obsessed with dazzling trinkets. Eventually, she learns her mysterious stranger is a demon spewed from the depths of Hell.

"Sadly, it is too late and she is caught between a rock and a hard place... literally. Girl can no longer take being whored out, especially when the aforementioned demon spawn wants the girl to find another to replace her.

"Girl destroys mysterious stranger's abode and escapes into the night with nothing but the proverbial coat on her back.

"End of story."

Thomas analyzed the tale she wove.

"Your stranger sounds like a real bastard. Did he do that to your hand?" He nodded to her palm. She had forgotten that part. "It looks pretty ugly, whatever it is."

"You are no better at this game, Thomas." Sela chided. She glanced at her hand then closed it quickly. "This... this is nothing more than a reminder of what happens when you put too much faith into anything or anyone."

"We all bear our scars, Sela. Some are more visible than

others," Thomas offered in priestly solace. "What are your plans now?"

Composing herself, Sela drained her mug. "Well, I was about to thank you for your kindness and be on my way. The snow has stopped and I have things to which I must attend,"

"So basically, you intend to live rough, surviving God knows how. What kind of priest would I be if I let you do that?"

Spotting Sela open her mouth to deliver a smart response, he hurried on, "I have a better idea. As you can tell by the conditions of my humble abode, I'm in need of a housekeeper. It's not a glamorous life, but it will keep you off the streets and out of my donation bin... well maybe."

While the offer was inviting, Sela had no desire to be tied or beholden to anyone, neither was she satisfied his motives were altruistic.

That said, wandering through the city aimlessly, looking for Peer is not an attractive alternative, either. Besides, here was the last place Peer would think to look.

As she pondered her next move, she felt a searing sensation in her palm. It was so intense, her hand opened involuntarily.

She closed it hastily when she saw the ugly scar of the coin appear to spin within her flesh.

If she was not going to make the right decision, Loki appeared content to do it for her.

In desperation she stared at Thomas, struggling to speak, but was rendered mute by the firestorm of pain spearing her palm.

Helplessly, she watched Thomas grab her wrist to unfurl her trembling fingers.

As he unclenched her fist, the pain subsided as quickly as it had started. The scar was unchanged; the coin's head seared into her palm, but a faint odor of charred flesh greeted the pair.

She yanked her hand out of his grip and rose from the table.

Sure of what she had seen, she surmised Loki had a use for the priest and leaving was not an option.

Regaining her poise, she ran her fingers through her hair, twisting it up into a bun, which also gave her the opportunity to wipe the beads of sweat from her brow.

"It looks like you have somebody to clean up after you, Thomas," she capitulated in grumpy resignation.

The once powerful queen had hit rock bottom. Supreme ruler, to bound whore, to kitchen slave.

There was a saying about the mighty and their eventual downfall, but she pushed away the adage, to collect the dishes from the table.

"So, if you do not mind, Priest, I have a sink full of dishes to wash."

Thomas stopped her.

"No, Sela, those can wait for the time being. Let me show you where you'll be staying and organize some clothes more suited to the position. I'm afraid they're less stylish than what you are wearing now, but they'll help you blend in. Besides, if the Cardinal were to stop by, I don't think he would be too happy about you being dressed like—"

"Like what?" Sela challenged.

"Like we just climbed out of bed," he chuckled.

"You should be so lucky," she retaliated, hands on hips.

Bracing himself for a ticking off, Thomas slipped a hand through Sela's crooked arm, and led her out of the kitchen to a small room at the end of the hall.

For some reason, Sela found comfort in the modest furnishings within. A narrow bed and night table hugged the far wall. A chair and table, opposite.

"Afraid it's not The Four Seasons, but it's snug. You'll find the housekeeper's uniform in the closet. Hopefully, it will fit. Mrs. Beale was about your height, but..." Thomas started, then hesitated not quite sure how to phrase what he wanted to say without causing offense, "... not quite as... shapely."

Who wants a room that follows the cycle of the year? Puzzled, but masking it well, Sela laughed softly. "I am sure I shall manage."

"Feel free to *borrow* whatever clothes you need from the bin, for when you are off duty. Sorting the donations is now part of your responsibilities, anyway."

Thomas paused at the threshold.

Before Sela had a chance to make a snide rebuttal, he added, "You'll find your coat in the closet. I'm not going to ask why two bullets are missing from the clip. I imagine that's a story I *don't* want to hear."

SEVEN

Sela assumed the role of housekeeper with aplomb, surprising herself, while inwardly thanking her mother for insisting her daughter learn to maintain a dwelling.

The uniform, while not the battle gear she was accustomed to, was not as bad as he had implied, and reminded her of the clothing worn by the women of her village.

The tan skirt, simple and plain in design, fell below her knees. The tunic was similarly modest, but in a darker shade. Both had necessitated an immense amount of tailoring.

Sela murmured her thanks to her long-dead mother for teaching her to sew. Clearly, whoever this Mrs. Beale had been, she enjoyed her food.

To the chagrin of the priest, Sela chose to crop her auburn tresses.

It made sense to her and, as she explained to Thomas, "It will be a nuisance bundling my hair up every morning to stuff it into a headscarf, and there's nobody around worth the effort required to brush it out."

Sela did not miss the flicker of disappointment in the priest's eyes at her cynical observation.

In truth, her decision to change hairstyle was because without her long flowing locks, she would be less vulnerable in a deadly struggle with Peer — should her nightly hunts ever bear fruit.

She was impressed at the speed with which Thomas had her position sanctioned through the myriad diocesan departments.

Earth or Hell, nothing could be confirmed unless it was signed in triplicate.

Thomas had created a suitable backstory in response to questions concerning her past. She wasn't sure why the priest was lying for her; but as long as it benefited her, she was not going to press him for details.

The elderly women in Thomas's parish took an immediate liking to her, relieved the bishop had seen fit to provide their beleaguered shepherd with a housekeeper, finally... and such a pretty one at that.

While they sorted through the donations, Sela listened to church gossip, nodding, and smiling where appropriate.

The women teased her gently about her delightful accent, remarking how it reminded them of people with whom they grew up, but she was careful not to slip into her native tongue... *and they make fun of how* I *speak.* Sela found *their* New York accent far harder to grasp. It was difficult to master, and trying to decipher its nuances resulted in splitting headaches.

Nevertheless, she persevered.

At coffee mornings, she ignored the salacious whispers of their husbands, jealous they did not have such an attractive young thing living with them. They might not care whether Sela heard, but took measures to ensure their wives did not.

Adjusting to twenty-first-century life as a whole, was Sela's greatest challenge.

While magic was practiced to a certain extent by the women of her day, nothing prepared her for what she encountered now.

Determined to become proficient in understanding and manipulating the profusion of bizarre contraptions beloved of this era, not to mention the subtleties of the language, and the specifics of this city, she exploited every resource available to her.

This *did* lead to some hilarity, but everyone was patient and most blamed her confusion on cultural variations.

Thomas *was* moved to wonder whether it had been a wise decision to give Sela free rein of his library given she took gleeful delight in employing Shakespearian insults at every opportunity.

Nevertheless, she was a quick study and soon, she was speaking English like a local.

Each new discovery, which for her was akin to a gift from Odin himself, appeared little more than an everyday nuisance to those around her.

She watched in wonder as people communicated through tiny flat boxes, they seemed tethered to permanently.

Thomas had insisted she carry one in case of emergencies, and no amount of reassurance that she could take care of herself, appeased him. In the end, she had acquiesced to curb his constant nagging.

She found one good use for it.

A neighborhood kid had shown her how it could play

music, and she enjoyed being able to ignore Thomas by listening to something called Death Metal.

It evoked the din of battles which, strangely, soothed her, and drowned out whatever he was blathering about.

Music was also a welcome companion when she disappeared into the city to hunt for Peer; the nights she perceived his energy intensifying, daring her to find him.

Another useful tidbit the kid taught Sela was something he called GPS.

As a child, her father had taught her to be a skilled tracker, a talent she had honed in the snowy woods of the north. In the concrete forest of this city, however, it proved useless, leading her to get lost far too easily, allowing Peer to elude her.

The knowledge he was just beyond her peripheral vision exacerbated her frustration.

This cat and mouse drama had become a game to Peer. One where he dictated the rules, as well as the playing field.

He took pleasure in compelling her to explore every sordid bar or kink club he could imagine.

One night, he decided to insult Sela's sense of taste by leading her to a hole-in-the-wall mead house a few blocks off Times Square.

Unlike the other taverns she had visited, this place had a distinctly different feel to it. She discerned Peer's presence even before she set foot inside but, when she opened the door, his spirit evaporated.

His abrupt disappearance made Sela question whether

everything she had experienced since her arrival in New York was the truth, or mounting exhaustion from the endless nights spent roaming Manhattan's streets.

Why would Peer bother with **this** *dump? I know he delights in his twisted follies, but...*

Not finding him in the crowd, Sela exhaled a small sigh of disappointment, although was not unduly surprised. She doubted even Peer would lower himself to cavort with the walking dead congregating here; the dark and musty interior, reflective of the class of patrons scattered about.

The scantily clad, half-starved urchins, gyrating against the pole on the stage, barely warranted Sela's swift, malicious glance as she perched on a bar stool.

Scoffing inwardly, she reassured the valkyries serving in Valhalla they had no fear their duties would be usurped by this lot.

The popularity of these clubs baffled Sela.

She understood the attraction of naked girls dancing on a raised platform for the gratification of men, but these females had no sexual magnetism; they were too scrawny.

Then there was the lack of decent ale, due in no small part to the City's by-laws pertaining to alcohol and strippers — a rule, Sela deemed pointless.

Are the men of this era too meek for carousing? Wine, women, and song... have they lost that tradition here? How sad.

There was nothing to redeem this particular establishment... *so why did he lead me here? I'm sure this bar, like all the others, will not serve a drink strong enough to wash away the sour taste in my mouth.*

Perhaps the masters of this city did not want their subjects to relax and celebrate their triumphs. Maybe, they feared it would lead to a skirmish.

She nodded shrewdly. The men of this century must be

too weak to handle their drink and their women at the same time.

"Yeah, I know they're not much to look at, but at least the alcohol isn't too watered down. What can I get ya?"

Sela snapped out of her thoughts.

A tall, good-looking man was leaning on the other side of the bar. She gave his six foot one frame the once over.

Even in the dimly lit bar, his eyes captured her attention. They seemed to sparkle in the spotlights of the stage show.

He sported what, Sela presumed the man believed qualified as a beard, although to her was barely chin stubble.

Has Odin cursed all of these men with the inability to grow a full beard?

She shrugged with a smile. "I thought the city frowned on getting your customers drunk in the presence of women?"

"If you don't tell, I won't either," the bartender pledged.

"Fine. Let's make it your choice, though. Preferably something to forget another waste of a night."

The bartender chuckled, "Well, that requires me to break out my drink app, but let's see what I can come up with."

Instead of reaching for the standard fare that lined the shelf, he gathered a handful of bottles from under the bar.

Catching Sela's quizzical look, he clarified, "Private stock. You don't expect me to drink the crap I serve this lot, do you?"

"Wasn't aware you were drinking with me," Sela retorted.

"Not often a beautiful, fully dressed woman comes into my bar. Figured, what the hell. It was worth a shot, but if you insist on drinking by yourself..." he trailed off, curious to see the woman's reaction.

"Well, since you have started brewing your concoction, who am I to refuse? Besides, I assume your attempt at a compliment means you're paying for the drinks?"

"Then maybe I should stick to the house stock," he countered.

"Do that, and you'll have zero chance of getting me drunk." Sela winked.

The bartender was enjoying their banter.

Beauty, brains, and *an attitude.* This one was definitely going to end up in his bed tonight.

"Well, if I'm gonna get you drunk, maybe I should find out who to call a cab for? I'm Nate, by the way."

"Nice to meet you, Nate. Finish pouring me a drink and perhaps I'll consider reciprocating," Sela sassed.

Nate set two shot glasses on the bar while Sela turned to watch the dancers work the stage, amused when she heard him pour extra in one glass. Without speaking, she reached behind to take the drink, swallowing it in a single gulp.

Spinning around, she slammed the glass upside down on the counter.

"Oh, how rude of me," Sela laughed softly, "I finished before you... that's a first. Pour me another and let's see whether you can catch up."

Arching his brow, Nate tossed back his half shot, then righted Sela's glass, impressed by how this woman could handle her liquor.

He was skeptical she would be able to keep it up, never mind drink him under the table.

Nate raised his glass in a toast. "*Skál!*"

Taken aback, Sela dipped her head. "*Skál!*"

Over the next few hours, matching each other drink for drink, the two chatted about nothing of any importance, trading jokes and observations about the clientele, while draining a bottle of top-shelf vodka.

"So much for the profits tonight. You could at least make my loss worthwhile and tell me your name," Nate implored, cracking the seal on an expensive bottle of Canadian whiskey.

"Since you've been such a gracious host, it's Sela." Her words colored by the warmth of the alcohol.

"Wow, that's different. I was pegging you as a Summer or a Laynee... with the emphasis on the double *ee*'s."

Nate's usual suave eloquence had been obliterated with his last shot and, well, she did have a nice rack, he thought, and she hadn't slapped his face... yet.

Sela downed her drink and set the glass on the bar. She was a trifle disappointed, if not concerned, at the amount of alcohol it had taken to feel even the slightest effect.

Has my time in Hell... Niflheim... caused any other physical changes? I guess there is only one way to find out.

"Look, Nate, it's late and I can't afford a cab home so how about we go to your place?"

Nate nearly dropped the bottle of whiskey.

He had given up on the idea of getting this woman into bed a couple of hours ago.

Nate boy, it looks like your luck might have changed.

Tossing his apron to one of the waitresses, he begged her to close up, promising she could take the next day off... with pay if she agreed.

The woman sent Sela a cursory glance, and shrugged. "Toss in the tips I'm gonna miss out on and we have a deal."

Nate all but leaped over the bar before the waitress

could rescind. Hooking Sela's arm through his, he tried to regain his composure as he escorted her to the door.

The waitress called after the couple, "Don't catch anything."

Sela was not sure who she was warning.

EIGHT

Exiting the club, Nate gave Sela a cheesy smile. "I was raised to come to the rescue of damsels in distress. Chivalry and all," trying not to slur his words.

Smacked in the face with the cold night air, Nate sobered up quickly. Shaking off the chill, he assured his houseguest, "I live around the corner so the damn winter won't kill the mood."

Sela, entranced by the number of people wandering the streets, scarcely registered his efforts at charming conversation, oblivious to the possibility they could be held up before reaching Nate's apartment.

Nate, cognizant of how dangerous this neighborhood could be, glanced at Sela, who looked more like a child watching a circus than an adult who ought to be leery of her surroundings.

He tightened his grip on her arm as they entered the alley which led them to Nate's door. An unnecessary gesture, given Sela showed not one iota of fear.

He sized her up, fumbling with his keys. *How drunk was she?* Her enthusiasm seemed to be waning.

Hold on, woman. Nate grumbled inwardly. *For what you've cost me in alcohol, you'd better be worth the fuck.*

Sela questioned whether this was a huge waste of her *first* time. Snatching the key, she unlocked the door and pushed it open. If knowing whether she could feel like a complete woman again had not become so inexplicably important, she would have told him she had lost interest.

She muttered under breath in Norse as he escorted her inside, "I hope you do not always have that much trouble finding the right keyhole."

"Wud ya say?" Flummoxed, Nate stared.

"Nothing. I'm just concerned you might have a problem with locks once we get to your place."

Even though centuries had passed since she was a queen, Sela felt she deserved a modicum of respect.

Do I not? At least to have sex with somebody who is capable of opening a door.

Watching her expression, Nate suspected he was blowing his chance. *I'm gonna risk a quick fondle before she walks.*

Daringly, he cupped Sela's supple ass, giving it a tender squeeze to test her mood, relieved when she didn't object.

Sela, busy convincing herself she had more important plans to which she ought to be attending, barely registered his advance.

Any small talk the two might have indulged in on the way up to his apartment was curtailed when Sela stopped him on one of the dimly lit landings.

Pushing him against the wall, she kissed him with all the pent-up passion, she thought lost beyond recall.

Since losing her virginity in a gang rape as a teen, the only male she had slept with was Peer. He had taught her all she knew about sex but, of late, she had begun to speculate some of his lessons probably constituted abuse rather than lovemaking.

She banished the thought. Tonight was not the time for introspection. Tonight was for scratching an itch, for testing a theory, made all the more gratifying because Nate was good-looking, and clearly wanted her.

Her kiss was the invitation he needed.

Shuffling them around until Sela was the one with her back to the wall, he crushed his lips to hers, their tongues tangling in an erotic dance. The sweet taste of her mouth mingled with the remnants of vodka and whiskey was an intoxicating combination.

His hands skimmed under her top to caress her breasts, savoring the sensation of her pert nipples against his palms. His lips scorched a path from her mouth to her throat, relishing the fact that she tilted her chin up to expose her neck.

In that split-second, Sela froze, certain she caught sight of Peer's stony gaze watching her from the corner of the ceiling, a sadistic grin contorting his face.

She glared at the shadow, her expression announcing — as clearly as though she had bellowed it in his ear — that what she was about to do was of her volition, and had nothing to do with him.

Visibly uncomfortable with Sela's new independence, Peer vanished.

Free of the specter, Sela, in her relief, attributed it to nerves… ignoring the sardonic laugher echoing in her mind.

Quelling an urge to flee, Sela speared her fingers into Nate's hair and lifted his head. She wanted to be anywhere but where they were standing.

Panting, she pleaded, "That was just an appetizer. Let's get to your place and check out the main course." She managed a saucy smile, willing him to take her out of the stairway.

Nate did not notice her half-hearted effort. Seizing her hand, he pulled her up the last two floors to his apartment.

This time, he had no problem with the lock — to Sela's well-concealed amusement. He yanked her inside and, kicking the door shut, pressed her flush to the wood paneling, covering the slender column of her throat with kisses.

Sela's mirth fled as she tugged Nate's shirt up over his back, her nails digging into his flesh, leaving red streaks, taunting him with a grind of her hips. Her lissome body, tortuous temptation.

Never relinquishing her mouth, Nate walked Sela backwards down the hallway. The pair stumbled, hands searching, as Nate steered them towards his bedroom, clothes littering the floor in their wake.

They reached Nate's bed. Sela stood before him naked, aware her body bore scars from centuries-old battles, for which she had no plausible explanation.

Reflexively, she covered herself and turned from his assessing gaze, suddenly unsure whether she wanted this to progress.

To compound matters, her heart drummed an erratic tattoo as memories of her traumatic ordeal at the hands of the damned, flooded her.

Should she run? Was that playing into Peer's han...

"God, you are beautiful."

The reverence in Nate's tone interrupted and banished her doubts as he enfolded her in his arms.

She bestowed on him her most bewitching smile.

Determined not to lose this opportunity; Nate gathered her against his hard body. His warm breath grazed her ear. "Quit toying with me, babe, you know I want you."

He peppered kisses across the sensitive skin of her collar bone, nuzzling her neck as he slotted her voluptuous frame to his strapping one.

His body whispered that whatever had happened in her past, tonight was all that mattered.

A soft moan spilled over her lips.

He traced her shape, trailing ever lower. As heat spiraled out from her core, it came to Sela that, for the first time in a thousand ages of man, the hand touching her was not deformed by death and corruption.

The tips of Nathan's fingers kindled her arousal, delivering the answer she so desperately sought.

The backs of her knees hit the mattress.

As though she might shatter, Nate lowered her to the bed, pinning her arms above her head. Lazily, his tongue swirled around her breasts, his teeth grazing the hard peaks. Their eyes met, and he captured her lips in a searing kiss, which went on and on and on.

Her body hungering for more, Sela broke for air, and paused for one brief moment to look up at the man who was causing wave after wave of infinitesimal pulses to glissade down her spine.

Nate had ignited a craving as old as life itself, and she felt almost human again. Her smoldering desire intensified as her body undulated wantonly.

This was *her* time.

Time to indulge her needs, her wants. Time to experience all the passion she had been denied in Niflheim.

In one fluid movement, she tipped Nate onto his back. Now, *she* was in control. *She* possessed the power to decide how this would play out. A thrilling notion, heightening anticipation.

"God, you're driving me to distraction." Nate croaked,

Sela's provocative gyrations had him teetering on the brink. He ached to plunge into her... actually ached.

A husky laugh rolled from her throat.

"Isn't that the point?" She tapped his chest. "And not yet. Not until I'm ready." She shimmied along his body shamelessly, her mouth and her fingers stoking the flames, the conflagration hovering just out of reach.

"When *I'm* ready," she murmured into his ear and bit the soft lobe, feeling him shudder underneath her.

She brought him tantalizingly close, over and over again, building to a crescendo, until he swore, he was going to explode, then — with a coy smile — she impaled herself on him.

At the sharp pain, Sela gasped a silent prayer to Odin that this would free her of the demonic curse of eternal maidenhood.

Through the maelstrom he now called his brain, Nate was stunned. The guys at the club would never believe he had just claimed this crazy beauty's virginity, but it was something he would never forget.

Before he was able to conjure any further coherent thought, Sela, in no mood to let this euphoria end too soon, began to weave her special brand of magic all over again, and the night disappeared in a journey of wild abandonment.

Revived, Sela was insatiable, taking hours to rediscover what she believed Peer had ruined forever.

In the aftermath, Sela lay in Nate's arms, reveling in the knowledge a male found her desirable, as well as enthralled by the realization she was capable of enjoying sex. The pertinent deity who had permitted *that*, deserved a heartfelt thank you.

She waited until she was sure Nate was deep in slumber. A wry grin twitched at her lips. Even now, males were unable to stay awake after sex; some things never changed.

Hearing Nate's measured snores, Sela slipped from his bed and padded through the apartment, collecting her discarded clothes, impressed at how far some had been flung.

Dressed, she ensured her pistol and phone were in the inner pocket of her coat, chuckling quietly over the fact Nate was too busy getting her in bed to notice she was armed. Mind, the gun might have added an interesting twist to their uninhibited coupling.

Returning to the bedroom, Sela studied Nate's sleeping form. Leaning over, she brushed a gentle kiss to his forehead. This would be the first and last time they met. "Goodbye, Nate," she said under her breath, and crept out.

No sooner had she closed the apartment door, than her phone chimed. She looked at the number half expecting it to be the priest — he was such an old woman about her whereabouts at this time of night — but this was a number she didn't recognize.

"Who in Odin's name is..." she scowled. Expecting it to be Peer encouraging her to embrace the whore within, the voice she heard took her by surprise.

"Was that actually necessary, Ms. Helsdatter?" It was the voice from the park.

"As a matter of fact, it was." Sela glared at the phone. "As I am responsible for resolving this challenge you set me... discovering how human I am was an essential exercise. I hope you enjoyed watching, by the way.

"And while I have your attention. Why did you leave me in a snowy park with no clothes? More importantly, if you want me to destroy Peer, given you must know where he is skulking, would it not be easier to tell me? It would save a whole lot of time and energy."

The response to her tirade was silence.

Her phone went dead. She scrolled through for the number but it was not listed in her recent calls. Roughly, she shoved the phone into her coat pocket and descended the stairs to the street.

Sela promised herself, once she had rid the world of Peer, Loki and she would be having words.

CHAPTER

NINE

As the days dragged on without any result, Sela began to wonder if she had actually escaped Hell... no Niflheim — the designation seemed to be one and the same in this era — or whether all she had done was to create another, less bleak version.

For nearly a month, Peer had not stalked her dreams, and she had not received any mysterious calls. Her nocturnal hunts dwindled because her lack of success exacerbated her frustration and she feared she was becoming sloppy.

She *had* discovered another modern miracle, more captivating than the music player on her phone.

Television.

While it offered her the opportunity to glean an inordinate amount of information about the world around her... including the mysterious *Mayan Calendar* referred to by the 'voice'... she was more entertained by watching people doing things which, she reckoned, would make even Loki blush.

While Thomas frowned, or tutted, or made some inane

comment about the end of man's morality and fall to sin, he usually ended up on the couch watching with her.

During one of these forays into the box of endless wisdom, she happened across a reporter interviewing a distinguished-looking gentleman in dark glasses who possessed a unique collection of ancient Norse armament and armor. Sela thought his dark eyewear, odd but it was television and who could say what was normal? She was more interested in the exhibit.

As the camera panned along the collection of swords, Sela was saddened to see the fate of the once prized weapons.

Such blades were passed from father to son, and it was considered a tragedy of catastrophic proportions if they were lost or stolen. Here, they were reduced to window dressing.

Although most had suffered irreparable damage — razor-sharp edges battered and splintered from battle, or rusted from their sacred burial — a handful had escaped the ravages of the centuries. Those swords gleamed as brightly as the day the blacksmith had — with justifiable pride — presented the fruits of his labor to the new owner .

Sela stopped listening to the gentleman pontificating about the difficulty in amassing his collection... until he lifted a particular sword from its case. The camera's light reflected off the metal, capturing Sela's full attention.

She knew this blade. The hilt was worn from being smashed with lethal efficiency against an opponent's skull during battle. The crucible steel which had been imported from lands far to the East, though nicked along the edges, still bore the mark of *Ulfberht* near the hilt.

*It was **her** blade.*

This sword and its mate had cost her dearly, but proved

worth their weight in the silver she had paid. Unlike Peer, they never failed her in battle.

She scoured the screen for the second sword, but the camera did not return to the display.

She listened more intently to the gentleman in hopes of garnering clues as to the whereabouts of her matching sword, but he was too busy waxing lyrical about the supposed legend of its owner. As the man prattled on, he replaced the blade in the case... *alongside its twin.*

Tears spilled down Sela's cheeks as the camera flashed one last shot of her precious swords, aware of Thomas's confused gaze as she wept at the television. She ignored him because what she saw next left her ashen and speechless.

When the camera panned to the gentleman for his closing remarks, his dark glasses were swinging nonchalantly in his hand. Peer smiled broadly at the fluff reporter while she flirted with him about how secure he must feel with so many weapons to protect him.

Peer appeared to spill beyond the edges of the screen to dominate the room she was in. His hollow eyes bore directly into Sela.

"I've grown tired of this game, Sela. It is time to end this, but I shall not make it easy for you, witch. Come see me."

The story switched from the swords to the weather forecast, but Sela's blank gaze remained fixed on the television.

Her hatred for Peer cascaded from her as she, only half-silently, hissed every Norse curse she could think of at the image of him branded into her brain. It wasn't until Thomas put his hand on her arm that she snapped out of it.

"What is it, Sela? You're as white as a sheet, and

muttering gibberish. You know my Norwegian sucks," Thomas exclaimed.

She arched an irate brow. "It doesn't concern you, Priest." Immediately contrite when she saw hurt, quickly masked, contort his face at her terse response.

That Thomas seemed unafraid to show his emotions, however briefly, was something Sela found hard to equate with what she knew of men. In her time, any inkling of sentimentality was ridiculed as a sign of weakness. She studied him, her head on one side... it was a refreshing trait.

"Forget it. I've got things I have to take care of," she tried to deflect as she got to her feet, her mind whirring with how she was going to recover her blades, then remove that reptilian grin... and the rest of Peer's head with them.

Then what?

Maybe she would mount Peer's ugly mug like a hunting trophy. Maybe Odin himself would shower her in gold for ridding his realm of the monster.

Maybe...

As she mused over a world without Peer, she felt a firm hand pull her back to the couch.

The mewl which arose from her throat resembled that of a wounded animal protesting its impending demise. Her eyes blazed at Thomas, and her hand whipped up to slap his face.

He grabbed her wrist mid-swing. His speedy reaction startled her.

Damnit, Priest, how are your reflexes sharper than mine? You should be wearing my handprint on your cheek.

"If you're done with your childish nonsense, perhaps you will let me know why the picture of that man and those swords upset you so badly. Maybe then, we can have an adult conversation about why they are, apparently, so important to you and see how we go." Not bothering to mask his exasperation

Sela's infuriated glare prompted him to add, "At the risk of personal injury to myself, I'm going to release your hand. I'm warning you, though, if you contemplate a repeat of that temper tantrum, it'll be the last thing you do tonight."

Holding Sela's gaze until she inclined her head, Thomas unfurled his fingers.

Rubbing the tender joint, she scowled. "You really need to work on your people skills, Priest."

"Yeah, I skipped that lecture during training. Tell me about the swords."

Sela took a steadying breath, willing a credible story to pop into her brain. She had to thank Public Television for the one she invented.

"That sword is one of a pair which belonged to my ancestors since the beginning of time, if you believed my grandmother. Anyway, my family still lived in Norway when the Germans invaded in World War II.

"As they did with anything of significant value, the Germans confiscated the swords, probably destined for Berlin, or Hitler's Führermuseum in Linz, Austria... that was the rumor.

"My great grandparents joined the resistance, determined to drive out the invaders, and then attempt to recover lost treasures.

"Regrettably, even after the Nazis were hounded out of Norway at the end of the war, there was no trace of the swords, or the countless other appropriated heirlooms belonging to my fellow countrymen."

Sela contrived to shed a few more tears in an attempt to sell her story, but Thomas listened without showing a shred of emotion.

She could not decide whether he believed her, and was not sure it mattered.

As if a hand had smacked the back of her head, it came to her that having an ally to support her was immeasurable, especially faced with the odds she was about to confront.

If she had learned anything in her numerous campaigns, it was that lesson. It was of utmost importance that he *did* believe her.

"Shortly after the war, my great-grandfather received a letter from the Art Looting Investigation Unit, stating the swords were listed on an inventory of some museum in Central Germany which had been obliterated in an Allied bombing raid, and how sorry they were for the loss… blah, blah, blah.

"They thought that was that and, although they mourned the loss of the blades, thankful to have survived the war, my family went on with their lives.

"My grandmother met my grandfather and they moved to America to raise a family."

Sela fell silent, staring at the screen but seeing a completely different picture.

Thomas presumed the story ended there, until Sela groused, glaring at the television.

"Whispers concerning the whereabouts of the swords surfaced over the next seventy years. The main one being that the blades weren't destroyed in the bombardment, but had been recovered by the Americans who were able to distinguish the symbol of the swords' maker.

"Of course, the rumor also said they had been auctioned off on the black market.

Sela brushed away her tears with the back of her hand, and sighed wistfully, "My family died without knowing the truth and now…"

"That was the worst story I've ever heard, Sela," Thomas raised his hand to stop her. "Next time you fabricate a tale, make sure I wasn't watching the same documentary."

He gave a long-suffering eye roll. "Ok… for argument's sake, let's say, I accept your word that these weapons mean something special to you and you want them back. The look on your face tells me, you are contemplating something rash. What if, between us, *we* formulate a plan to retrieve them?

"Although, before we do, have you considered legal means? There must be a thousand lawyers in this city, dredged up from Hell, ready to leap at the chance to represent a *beautiful, young woman, wronged by a wealthy, yet unscrupulous collector holding her ancestral swords hostage.*"

Sela blushed at Thomas's description.

Accustomed to the older women of the church flattering her, this was the first time Thomas had done so. She shook it off. This was not the time to get involved with him or any man.

Sela was also uncomfortable with his interpretation of the situation.

Have I said too much? Has he deciphered the truth behind my presence?

She tried to recall their conversations, but nothing stood out. She knew there were things which perplexed him; her nightly expeditions, the evening they met, the gun…

She would deal with that later… if she had to.

"Look, Thomas, we both know there are bad people in this world who act outside the confines of the law. No matter how many lawyers you throw at them, it's never enough. This man wields an evil all his own. The only way I can reclaim what's rightly mine, is by force."

"So, without doing any reconnaissance, or having a strategy, or taking back up, you're going to storm the castle?"

With a single question, Thomas made Sela feel like an impetuous child for entertaining the idea.

"How about considering a different approach? What if a humble priest was to visit this character in the guise of soliciting support for a local charity, during which he gains a clearer layout of his collection?"

His suggestion had potential, but Sela did not want him caught up in her quest. While he might be blessed with guile, persuading people to untie their purse strings was child's play compared with the artifice required to deal with Peer. It was unfair to expect the priest to compromise his calling to help her.

"I couldn't possibly get you involved in this, Thomas. Any slip and this man would have no compunction killing you, and take great pleasure in doing so," Sela tried to discourage him, though it was half-hearted at best, because he was right.

She needed more information about Peer's shack... hovel... castle... whatever.

The television report gave no indication as to the size of the place. On top of this, Peer expected her now, meaning a direct attack was out of the question.

"I'm a big boy, Sela," Thomas reassured. "I can charm and disarm when necessary." His hand came to rest on Sela's thigh. "If I can squeeze a few shekels from him, all the better."

Her employer's almost chameleon-like capacity to slide from happy-go-lucky priest to humble supplicant, never ceased to impress Sela. Unapologetically wearing his heart on his sleeve while, perhaps, leaving him vulnerable to censure, also meant people trusted him implicitly.

Sela attributed this ability to manipulate the emotions of others to something he was taught by his elders at the Seminary he kept talking about.

Her eyes shifted from his face to his hand, which she moved, delicately, back to his knee. Relief she had help, did not mean letting him get chummy.

"Don't say you weren't warned. If you are sure you want to risk it, we have to figure out how to get you a meeting with him."

The duo spent the next few hours scheming.

Thomas was correct; a priest could show up, unannounced, on the doorstep of some city high roller who might be persuaded to make a donation, especially as he had just been on television.

The only question was *which charity?*

They were discussing this when the late news started. Expecting a rebroadcast of Peer's segment, Sela paid closer attention than was her habit.

As she surmised, the story was repeated.

During the reporter's introduction of Peer, Sela was not surprised to learn he had updated his name to Peter Bjorg.

He was, of course, too vain to choose a completely different name, and only Peer had the effrontery to call himself Peter the *Savior*.

She shook her head in disgust.

Savior being a relative concept. He would save them alright, then deliver them straight to that infernal rock in Nifl... Hell.

While, to outward appearances, the broadcast was exactly as it had been earlier, Sela perceived a subtle change.

Focusing on Peer's words, Sela noticed he was provoking her deliberately. Goading her to make the first move.

Throughout the segment, it was as though his remarks were directed at her specifically, and she swore, he brandished the sword at the camera more frequently.

Thomas may not have detected the disparity, but Sela knew she was not imagining things.

Battling the urge to put her boot through the television, thanks to Peer's condescending voice and smarmy face, she pressed the off button.

"Did you learn anything new?" Thomas quizzed, as Sela frowned at the blank screen.

"Yeah, I learned that cretin hasn't reformed in all this time." Sela swallowed a sigh. "How are you at representing the plight of the prostitutes who roam this city? That's Peer's weakness, one you can play on," she volunteered flatly.

"Are you asking me to hire hookers to distract the man? I'm pretty sure the Cardinal won't authorize the expenditure for that," Thomas joked, in an effort to make Sela smile.

She met his glib comment with a bland stare. His attempt at humor was the last thing she could deal with right now.

"I recommend you come up with a feasible story tonight, as well as get a decent sleep. Everything depends on how well you pull this off, and I cannot afford any mistakes," she instructed as she stalked out.

Thomas heard her door shut with a loud bang.

Aware she might decide to prowl the streets in the darkness, he was equally determined she would not, and resolved to spend the night preparing a foolproof game plan, while ensuring Sela stayed put.

In her present state, she'll end up at this Peter's place before either of us is ready, and, she has made it clear, any mistakes by either of us could be the death of me.

Sela had no intention of leaving.

She sat on the edge of her bed, face buried in her hands, sobbing uncontrollably. She could not let Thomas see her weeping, not over two inanimate objects she once prized more than a village woman prized her offspring.

Especially when they both knew Peer was using them to draw her into a duel.

The incongruous timing of that annoying invisible voice reminding her not to harm an innocent only made matters more intolerable.

Sela was well aware of the danger she was putting Thomas in and she hated herself for it, but what was the alternative?

Besides, he *had* volunteered. She could not be held responsible for that, could she?

Even if she was finding herself falling in lo…

She couldn't bring herself to finish that thought. Too much was at stake. There would be time to worry about such things when this was finished.

Wouldn't there?

Sela studied the brand on her palm, sending out a silent plea, *is my decision the right one?*

She knew the answer before she felt the burn of the coin.

TEN

Even though February had yet to relinquish its grip on the calendar, the air bore distinct traces of March when Thomas alighted from the IRT at Hudson Station on 34th Street.

The weather had been unusually mild, and the last vestiges of dingy brown snow were melting from the streets of Manhattan.

The pair had spent an unsuccessful couple of days trying to locate the home address of this Bjorg character. The ultra-rich of New York were past masters at hiding in plain sight and for a demon of the underworld, it was child's play.

With barely a flicker of magic, Peer could conceal his home from prying eyes.

In desperation, Thomas had come up with the brilliant idea of reaching out to the bubble-headed reporter. Relying on his charm as a Catholic priest, he succeeded in wheedling the address out of her by dint of some shameless flattery, delivered with a lilting Irish brogue — faked, of course.

In return he promised her exclusive coverage of the Parish's Spring Carnival.

The time they waste on trivial things to flesh out the television schedule, Thomas thought cynically, and why people in this city assumed all priests had Irish ancestry, he could not fathom.

From what Sela had told Thomas about their target, it seemed fitting he would reside in the Chelsea neighborhood, whose historic district retained the olde-world charm of the original settlement. Georgian and Victorian architecture offering a quaint facade against the backdrop of the encroaching metropolis.

The district was rife with off-Broadway culture, complete with impressionable young actors, and only a stone's throw from Hell's Kitchen.

Sela found that coincidence particularly amusing. She did not explain why and Thomas had not bothered to ask.

It had taken all his powers of persuasion to extract Sela's word that she would stay at home.

She had been bound and determined to accompany him to confront — or rather — to meet their prospective benefactor, while playing the role of quiet, chaste housekeeper.

Sela tried to persuade Thomas her presence would assist his cover of fundraising. The image of a fallen wench's life turned around; the embodiment of what could be achieved with a little help.

Thomas refused to countenance that idea. He knew full well she would charge in with reckless abandon, and land them both in jail.

Nevertheless, he kept a sharp eye out, unable to shake the feeling of being hunted like a deer in the forest.

"Headstrong woman," he muttered as he reached Peter Bjorg's rowhouse.

Thomas had practiced his speech multiple times during the subway ride but, about to deliver it, questioned whether it sounded genuine.

Sending up a swift prayer, and mentally crossing his fingers, he climbed the steps and rang the bell.

After an uncomfortable interval when Thomas suspected his journey might have been for naught, the heavy oak door creaked open.

For a split-second, Thomas was uncertain whether he was being greeted by Mr. Bjorg or an extraordinarily well-dressed butler. Given the location, neither would have surprised him.

Even to Thomas's inexperienced eye — in fact, it would have been obvious to the blind that this was not some cheap, off-the-rack garment — the quality of the man's suit was one of which a Saville Row tailor would be proud.

Despite it being made of the finest fabric, Thomas got the peculiar impression it was akin to a suit of armor.

A flicker of unease trickled down Thomas's spine, exacerbated by the impression Bjorg had been waiting for this precise moment. The notion threatened to knock him off his game, but it was too late to abandon the idea.

The well-heeled homeowner broke the silence. "Ah, Padre, what brings you to my door this fine morning? I hope I haven't violated one of the commandments and am now facing eternal punishment."

"No, Mr. Bjorg, while the Lord works in mysterious ways, we haven't quite reached the point of instant retribution. That said, it is undertaking the Lord's work which has led me to your door in hopes of securing your support to save wayward souls."

Thomas heard the gentleman give a dry chuckle but, after a brief pause, he was ushered inside.

"Father Um…"

"Thomas… Thomas Lockwood," Thomas filled in the blank.

"By all means, Father Thomas, please elaborate. Lost souls always interest me," Bjorg's demeanor evoked a cobra poised to strike.

Standing in the foyer Thomas was held motionless, astounded by the immense proportions of the house, so much so, he was tempted to go back outside to check the exterior to see how it was possible.

His host's hand planted firmly in the middle of his back, urged him deeper into the residence, as Bjorg escorted Thomas to a room off the main hallway.

To describe the furnishings within the office as ostentatious was doing the room a disservice. Gilt-framed paintings and innumerable hunting trophies overwhelmed the walls in the name of decoration.

The dark wood paneling, while presumably the pinnacle of fashionable sophistication, sucked out any light which seeped in through the beautiful, arched, stained-glass windows, leaving the room grim and unwelcoming.

Bjorg paused to allow Thomas to marvel at the wealth on not-so-subtle display.

Satisfied the priest recognized his importance, Bjorg offered Thomas a comparatively modest, antique, wooden seat, before circling his desk to sink onto a pretentious, high-backed Victorian chair — the somewhat gothic style, akin to a throne.

The term 'desk' was almost a misnomer.

The massive mahogany monstrosity, complete with a ridiculous amount of ornate scrollwork, was designed to instill a sense of inadequacy into whoever had requested an audience.

It compelled anyone sitting opposite their host to crane their neck in order to see over the expansive, neatly organized, and highly polished surface. A deliberate ploy, no doubt.

The arrangement reminded Thomas of the numerous times he was called to Father Britton's office at the Seminary, to discuss his attitude and whether he ought to reconsider his future as a priest. Bjorg's humorless smile as he settled into his chair was similarly condescending.

"Now then, Father. How might a simple servant of the Lord and our fellow man be of help to your cause?"

It was all Thomas could do not to gnash his teeth at the patronizing charlatan.

Infusing every ounce of charisma into his voice, Thomas launched into his spiel, "I know turning up at your door unannounced was not only rude but also presumptuous. For that, I apologize sincerely. Sometimes you have to take a risk. As the saying goes: Nothing ventured, nothing gained—"

Bjorg interrupted, "Yes, yes, I'm familiar with the concept but I'm still not sure what this has to do with me?"

"Sir, my parish sponsors a shelter for women who have fallen victim to the predators stalking the streets. Imagine, if you will, a young girl coming to the big city, starry-eyed and full of dreams.

"No sooner off the bus from small-town America than her future is shattered, taken in by some scoundrel who sweeps her off her feet at the terminal and obliges her to sell her body, not to mention her soul, on a dingy corner, so she can eat.

She becomes a victim, trapped by an evil from which she can never escape." Thomas impressed himself with his delivery, but Bjorg's inscrutable expression did not alter. He had yet to be convinced.

With nothing to lose, Thomas forged ahead before Bjorg kicked him out.

"I can see why you might be confused, so permit me to clarify.

"I had the pleasure of watching your story on the news and thought someone with such zeal for preserving the treasures of the past, *had* to be a man who could not ignore the discarded of the present."

"I see," Bjorg's succinct reply gave nothing away as he leaned back, arms crossed in silent consideration.

In the time Thomas had spent hitting up these fat cats for money, unsuccessfully, it must be admitted, Bjorg's rigid posture was never a good sign. Had he brought a briefcase, he would be retrieving it, and apologizing for wasting the man's time.

Regrettably, he had no option but to sit tight, and wait for Bjorg to respond.

Minutes, which felt like hours to Thomas, ticked by.

Tapping his chiseled chin with his index finger, Bjorg spoke. "Let me see whether I understand this, Padre. You see me revealing my collection on television and think, 'There's an easy mark. I bet after a moving sob story, he'll cough up cash faster than a broken ATM.'

"Am I close?"

"Well," Thomas started, "I wouldn't put it quite…"

Imperceptibly his demeanor altered, discernible by the faintest suspicion of a smile. "Okay, you got me. It is a sin to lie, especially for a priest. Yes, it was *exactly* like that."

The man in the high-backed chair gave a bark of laughter at Thomas's honesty. "I must say, your adherence to your vows does you credit, Father Thomas. A lesser man would have continued lying to me and tried to kiss my ass for money."

"Sorry to disappoint you, sir, but ass has been off my diet for quite a while now." Thomas chuckled, relaxing as much as was humanly possible on the hard chair.

"Padre, you amuse me, but perhaps I can do better than simply handing you a check?

"What if I was to arrange a small gathering, here, with some of my more affluent friends and clients, and you charm them out of their hard-earned, inherited cash? Say this Friday? Or would that interfere with mass?"

The offer was too good to be true, and even if it did, Thomas could not say no because the church's coffers were in dire need of a boost. Exhibiting the cool head of a gambler unwilling to tip his hand, Thomas did not reply immediately.

This prompted an arched brow from Bjorg, who expected the priest to drop to his knees in effusive thanks for the opportunity. On the contrary, the man across from him appeared to be treating this as a business negotiation.

"Is there a problem, Padre?" Bjorg's question was colored with more than a modicum of irritation.

"My apologies, Mr. Bjorg. Your proposition is exceedingly generous. I was momentarily distracted by what your munificence affords," Thomas reassured him.

"Have you considered leaving the priesthood to seek employment in the private sector? I could use a man with your skill for arbitration in my company."

The man's tone was more than complimentary, it sounded like a genuine job offer.

"Thank you, Mr. Bjorg. I am flattered, but no. I'm afraid my present employer doesn't accept resignations quite so readily."

Bjorg stood. "A shame but, should your situation change..." he left that dangling, rounding the desk, arm extended, signaling an end to their discussion.

Thomas stared at the outstretched hand, scouring his brain for a way to complete the one task he had been sent here to accomplish.

"May I be so bold as to ask you to indulge me with one more favor, sir? One of a personal nature?" Thomas was pushing his luck but, if he didn't try, Sela's retribution would carry a sharper sting than his host's displeasure.

"Padre?" Bjorg's voice rose, unable... quite... to mask his increasing annoyance at being badgered by this random do-gooder.

It did not go undetected by Thomas, who strove to mollify. "I do not think the report did the elements of your collection justice. In my line of work, being a historian of sorts kinda comes with the territory. Would you honor me with a quick tour? I promise not to take up much more of your time."

The humble request struck a note with Bjorg. To flaunt his wealth and power was one of life's little joys, and who was he to deny a penniless priest a glimpse of what was attainable... had he taken him up on his offer?

He smiled and hauled his guest out of the chair.

"By all means, Padre. How remiss of me, not to show you the very thing that brought you to my door," Bjorg apologized as he escorted Thomas to the hallway and to a staircase which led the pair to a matched set of medieval-style oak doors.

Thomas watched the man produce a heavy iron key, apparently, from thin air.

Cheap trickery, Thomas thought cynically.

Bjorg pushed the doors open into another, inexplicably,

oversized room. Armored mannequins flanked the door, stood like silent sentries along the walls, and as guards at the ends of each display case.

It was the figures themselves, however, which made Thomas whistle.

The armor appeared to be in excellent condition, considering when each was crafted. Tragically, the same could not be said of the warriors, who seemed battle worn and weary; hair and beards, dirty and matted.

Nevertheless, they were posed as though awaiting a call to battle.

"I consider them my private army," Bjorg explained, proudly, breaking Thomas's scrutiny. "They may look like an overwhelming force but, if the history of the Norse has taught us anything, superior numbers don't always guarantee a victory."

Clearly obsessed by his acquisitions, Bjorg gave Thomas an exhaustive tour. The latter was more than receptive, committing the dimensions of the room and the placement of the cases to memory. He took special note of the two blades Sela was so intent on retrieving, pausing by the case a little longer than the others, prompting Bjorg to backtrack.

"Ah, Padre, I see you've discovered the pride and joy of my repository. These two blades have a checkered past, starting with their original owner.

"According to legend, they were treasured by a bloodthirsty, yet minor queen who lived in the ninth or tenth century. Seems her reign was distinguished by a series of conquests, until her disgruntled neighbors settled their own disputes and ended her gruesome trail of destruction on the chopping block.

"Perhaps there is a grain of truth in it, but you know

how stories are passed down and embellished with each telling. In fairness, their superior quality infers they belonged to someone of privilege.

"These would be costly weapons... and the marred edges suggest they were not merely ornamental."

Thomas rubbed his chin as he admired the sheen of the blades. "Why two? Wouldn't a pair be a hindrance to wield in a skirmish?"

Thomas could never be sure he heard the reply, "I taught her to become one with them, on the training ground, and in battle."

"I beg your pardon?" Thomas waited for him to repeat it.

Bjorg glanced at his watch and then at Thomas. "I said, I'm sorry to have to bring this tour to an end so quickly, but I have business which I have sorely neglected this morning. Besides, we can talk again at the soiree on Friday."

Hurriedly, he escorted Thomas to the front door. As they reached the entrance, Bjorg extended his hand once more. This time, Thomas accepted it and gave it a firm shake.

"Thank you for your time, Mr. Bjorg. You have been more than generous."

Still shaking Thomas's hand, Bjorg countered, "I probably wouldn't have given you the time of day, Padre, except when I opened the door, you seemed familiar. A notion which has increased throughout our brief acquaintance. I have a penchant for recognizing names and faces.

"I am certain we have met before."

Like Houdini from a straitjacket, Thomas extracted his hand from Bjorg's grip. The two men locked eyes and Thomas grinned, affably. "I doubt we have in this lifetime. Have a good day, sir."

He left Bjorg standing in his doorway, aware of the man's narrowed gaze boring into him, as he strode down the street.

Thomas did not glance back.

He rounded the corner and crossed to the next block, stopping at the entrance to a small alley. Leaning against the wall, he shook his head. "Whoever taught you how to trail a target needs to give you a refund."

Sela stepped from the shadows, a scowl on her face. "You had no idea I was following you until you left the house."

"You better hope Bjorg didn't see you. Otherwise, you might not be able to join me Friday for a private party in that fabulous house."

Sela gaped, slack-jawed, at the news. "***Really?***"

"Yep, the terrible man wants me to fleece his friends. How could I refuse?" Thomas teased.

Sela flung her arms around Thomas and hugged him, holding him a little longer than she ought. Thomas laughed inwardly at how people were having a hard time letting go of him this morning.

He allowed himself to relax and enjoy this beauty's warm embrace. Some days, being a priest could be a pain in the ass. He let that thought pass to concentrate on formulating a plan for stealing the blades.

"Ok, woman, it's time we go home so you can start raiding the donation bin again for something suitable to wear, then figure out how to disguise you enough to get in. I have no doubt *your friend* will be expecting your presence."

ELEVEN

In the two days since Thomas had pulled off the impossible by precipitating an official invitation into Peter Bjorg's home, the pair had mapped the layout of those areas of the house Tomas had been privy to, as closely as he could recall.

Sela admired his forethought in memorizing the number of paces to her blades. When she pressed him on what prompted that brainwave, he joked about being a pirate in a previous life.

If they survived this, she was *definitely* going to follow that up.

A mission for another day. Today's quest was to come up with a strategy for Friday, and given it was already Wednesday that took precedence over pirates and previous lives.

Sela's mind went off on a tangent... *did priests* have *previous lives?* Hmmm... something else to ponder.

Sela had eschewed sleep, preferring to apply her considerable intelligence to their gambit. In the end, when her mouth and her brain disconnected, Thomas dispatched her to bed, refusing to listen to her protests — muddled though they were.

Exhausted and stressed, Sela was unable to form a coherent argument. *War preparation is a game for a younger woman*, she mused with a half-laugh, as she stretched out on her bed, fully clothed.

Before she could be bothered to change into her pj's, sleep overtook her. Almost immediately, Sela realized her mistake... this wasn't slumber — it was darkness.

Sela stood motionless, *here we go again, really Peer?* Fury welled within her leaving no room for fear. Impatiently, she waited for her adversary to appear, only to become the one demanding *his* presence.

"Show yourself, Peer. I have no time for your ridiculous games."

"Sela, how angry you've become living among these wretched mortals," Peer's voice preceded him. "You once had the refinement and intelligence of a warrior queen and now—"

In the midst of Peer's criticism, she lunged forwards, hoping to catch him off guard during his tirade. She was left cursing under her breath when all she grasped was thin air.

Her feeble attack merely reinforced his disdain for her, and provoked a bout of derisive laughter.

"You ought to be ashamed, you demonstrate less finesse than the common whore you were born to be."

Ignoring his words and, umbrage thick in her voice, she exhorted, "Why have you summoned me to this dismal plane, Peer? Have you come to surrender and put an end to this madness once and for all? I should be exceedingly happy to kill you now."

"Tsk tsk. No, my beautiful piece of flesh, I thought you might be missing the abyss and needed a reminder of your eternal... unrest. Unless, of course, you are still open to my offer?"

"What? You think I am willing to lead your army into battle? As delusional as you might be, Peer, that proposal is long gone from the table. We both know how far I have fallen from your good graces. Neither do I have any intention of begging to return to your service," Sela sniped sarcastically.

"*Au contraire*, my love, I have found an eminently qualified replacement, although fortunately for him, he will not face an eternity bound to the stone as some toy for the dead. You did not expect me to wait forever for you to fulfill your end of the bargain, did you?" Peer said calmly.

"Amazingly, I found his ability to smooth-talk his way into getting what he wanted refreshing... not quite equal to my silver tongue, mind you... but enough to lead these sheep to their slaughter."

Sela froze. Peer meant Thomas,

Not wanting to divulge Thomas's name or his connection to her, she stammered, "Y-You cannot be serious, Peer. No sane man would follow you."

Peer's attention drifted beyond Sela, as though uninterested in anything *she* had to say.

Absently, he observed, "We both know these detestable mortals are on the path to their own destruction. Before they succeed, I wish to return to Helheim to assume my rightful place as *Yfirherra. Overlord.*

"If Odin leaves the worthless child of that idiot Loki to run the place, the unexpected influx of souls will overwhelm her. Her wanton meddling is out of control. Like father, like daughter, don't you think?"

Peer didn't wait to hear Sela's opinion. "Left to her own devices, Hel's foolish blundering will drive the realms of Yggdrasil to wrack and ruin just as she did with Nástrǫnd and Niflheim."

"Do you honestly believe Loki will sit back and let you harm his daughter?" Sela could not believe Peer, even with his over-inflated ego, possessed the audacity to lock horns with Loki.

"That old fool has reached the end of his trickery. Besides, I have plans for him once I have Helheim under my rule."

Peer's arrogance was more than Sela could handle. The outrage she had tried to suppress, erupted.

"If you want to get there so quickly, bring yourself to me, **now**. Stop with the theatrical sorcery and face me."

Sela took another swipe at Peer's image. It was a futile gesture, but watching him dissolve was gratifying.

He cackled scornfully, his parting remark echoing in the shadows as the void swallowed him. "I know you're coming for your precious swords, bitch. You had better hurry before I do to them what I did to your soul!"

"Don't you dare, you... you..." A litany of Shakespearian oaths, Sela — who considered them to be the most delicious part of the Bard's tales — had learned and committed to memory when trying to master the nuances of the English language, clawed for release. "...**pestilent, batfowling, canker-blossom.**"

Her ranting elicited a snide laugh from Peer.

In the real world, Sela was thrashing about on her bed.

Her screeched threats had disturbed Thomas. He burst into her room and, seizing her by the shoulders, shook her firmly, trying to wake her as he had the night in the bathtub.

Sela lashed out, battering Thomas with ferocious fists.

"Sela, snap out of it," Thomas commanded.

His voice pierced her torment, and her eyes flew open.

Spying the reddening skin her onslaught had inflicted, Sela buried her face in his chest and, clinging to him as though she would never let go, sobbed like a child.

"He knows I'm coming for the blades."

"Of course, he does, Sela. Why else did he show you them?" Thomas said, which did little to soothe her.

"How are we going to succeed if he's expecting us," Sela lifted her head to search Thomas's face.

It shocked her to find an indomitable strength. It was one she had not witnessed in any warrior before — not even Peer.

The impulse to kiss him was almost irresistible but, by sheer effort of will, she refrained, making do with nestling her head against his chest and listening to the erratic beat of his heart.

Thomas had no such qualms, and surrendered to the temptation he had been battling since first they met.

Gently, he tilted her face up. His lips grazed hers with a fierce tenderness, a tantalizing entrée to something infinitely more appetizing, hovering just out of reach.

Not only did it quench a rapidly intensifying urge, he hoped it might take her mind off the demon tormenting her.

The bewilderment in her blue eyes, still swimming with tears, informed him he had done the opposite.

Speechless, she gaped at him, then crumpled against his chest.

"Because we are smarter than he is, we know what he's

thinking and, as long as we stick to the plan, we can't fail." Thomas rested his chin on the top of her head, stroking her back.

"Try to get some rest. I doubt you will have another nightmare and, if you do, I'm right down the..."

"Stay, Thomas, please stay with me," Sela beseeched softly.

He hesitated, his heart and his brain argued the wisdom, or spectacular lack thereof, of consenting to her request.

A glance at her woebegone expression and, inevitably, his heart won. "Only until you fall asleep, Sela." he acquiesced and, after easing her onto the bed, he maneuvered his tall frame alongside to tuck her back to his chest.

Unable to help himself, he breathed in the essence of the woman in his arms. Thomas knew Sela didn't wear scent, but her natural fragrance was more intoxicating than anything contrived by the most skilled perfumer.

As Sela's breathing evened out, Thomas tried to untangle himself, but even in slumber she refused to let him go.

He was stuck.

Well aware the church would require him to say *Hail Marys* until the end of time for kissing Sela, Thomas decided a few more were worth the perceived sin of spending this night comforting a distraught woman... in her bed.

Shuffling to make himself as comfortable as possible, he prepared to join her in well-deserved rest.

His hand engulfed Sela's, he felt heat radiating from her palm. Lifting it slightly, he noticed the ugly disfigurement of the cursed scar appeared to glow brightly in the gloom, sure he spied specks of dried blood around the edges.

Sela whimpered in her sleep.

Bringing her hand to his lips, Thomas brushed a kiss across her knuckles. She wriggled, settling against him, their bodies curved together as though a single form.

Unbidden, Thomas was overcome with dread and a sense of foreboding, along with a yearning to protect Sela. An unfamiliar, almost visceral emotion, but one from which he did not shy. He would keep Sela safe, if it meant risking his own life.

"This may well be our only night together," Thomas murmured, unaware, until it was too late, he had spoken out loud.

"Then we should make the most of it," came the equally quiet response.

Sela shifted in his arms, until they faced each other.

Tracing his craggy jaw with light fingertips, she molded herself to him, sensing Thomas was about to list a million reasons why this was the absolute worst decision. Every last one — irrefutable.

With an impish lift of her chin, she offered herself to Thomas.

Running his fingers through her silken hair, Thomas captured her mouth, holding nothing back. He savored the taste of her, the feel of her nails digging into his skin, inducing him to deepen their kiss, as she opened to him, their tongues dueling for dominance.

Desperate hands stripped away clothing. Speed trumped elegance, their bodies undulating sinuously as they hurried to shimmy out of unyielding jeans, inflaming desire.

With the deftness of a magician, Thomas rid Sela of her top and bra.

Shivering a little in the cool air, Sela giggled, "Hopefully, not everything goes that quickly."

Thomas smiled down at her, "Eh, if it does, we'll just have to start all over again."

Looping her arms around his neck, Sela snuggled closer as their eyes locked for a long moment.

Then, with a sigh that seemed to come from a vast distance, he stole her lips in a kiss that went on forever.

An inner flame caught, flickered, and began to burn. She wanted him to take her now, but he was not ready to quench her thirst... not yet.

Slowly, and with consummate skill, he took his sweet time seducing her, making her writhe underneath him, leaving no part of her untouched, bringing her to the peak time and again, but refusing to let her fly.

The delicious prelude, hinted at a handspan of time ago, blossomed. Sela's heart thrummed, and blood pounded through her veins as the fire threatened to become a conflagration.

In all of her life, she had never had a man care about *her* pleasure.

Her introduction to sex was being handed around the invaders who had laid waste to both her village and her virginity.

Peer had made her climax but, in truth, he was more interested in slaking his own lust, than in satisfying Sela. Any rapture she derived from their frantic coupling was purely coincidental.

Chained to the rock, ecstasy had become the instrument of her eternal damnation, leaving her repulsed by what she had endured.

Even Nate didn't accommodate Sela's needs. Yes, he had been an eager partner, but his goal was sex followed by a great night's sleep.

Thomas was like no other man.

Masterfully, he wove his spell, bringing her to a blinding orgasm simply because he wanted to.

Before she could recover, he started again, causing her to scream out in unbridled passion.

Sela reciprocated with earth-shattering interest, until neither knew where one wave of euphoria ended and the next began.

Bodies convulsing, they rode the vortex down, gasping for air, trembling in the aftermath. Thomas enfolded Sela in his arms. Neither spoke, words were unnecessary, and would sound like empty promises.

Wrapped together, they slept.

TWELVE

When Sela awoke the next morning, she was alone, a state of affairs which suited her because she had no idea what to say to Thomas, or how to address what happened without sounding like a crazed loon or, worse, hurting him however inadvertently.

Slipping into a pair of sweatpants and a T-shirt, she padded into the kitchen.

That Thomas had been there earlier was evidenced by the half-pot of cold coffee and a note.

S,

Had to go to the Archdiocese to take care of some last-minute preparations for tomorrow's party. Sorry you missed breakfast, but you looked like you needed sleep. Anyway, I figured since the church is paying you to be a housekeeper, you could actually try your hand at it and maybe clean up.

Be back later.

T

"A true romantic," Sela scoffed as she tossed the note in the garbage. She poured the cold coffee into her mug, and took a gulp before contending with the menial task of cleaning the kitchen.

Her jaw dropped as she registered, Thomas must have used every dish in the house, as well as some she'd never seen before, to make breakfast. The place was a disaster and would take her hours to...

"*Fjandinn þér,*" she swore at the priest. *Damn you.*

Clearly, this was his idiotic scheme to keep her in the house while he was gone.

She had things to do this morning as well, and picking up after Thomas was not one of them.

Draining the last of the coffee, she tossed the mug in the sink, hearing an unmistakable tinkle when her ceramic cup landed on top of the clutter, and suspected at least one piece of crockery had met its doom.

Stalking out of the kitchen, Sela grabbed her coat and informed the empty house in a subdued roar, "Nice try. Clean up your own mess."

Collecting her purse, filled with the currency of this realm, or — as the people here called it, her wages — she left, slamming the front door as she went.

Although it made her feel better, she accepted it was futile, given Thomas was not at home to witness her reproof.

Sela's first visit was to a wig shop she had seen advertised on the television.

Located further downtown than she expected,

warranted a ride in one of those yellow boxes which nearly took her life, the night she arrived in this place.

Hiding her trepidation, she copied the gesture, Thomas used to flag one down, amazed when a driver brought his beast to a rapid halt right next to her.

Sela dithered at the rear door, *how did this thing operate, again?* Whenever she accompanied Thomas, he had opened the door for her. His chivalry meant she was currently at a loss.

"Lady, are you getting in or not?" the driver asked brusquely.

"Yes, I wish for you to take me to this address," Sela replied, waving the torn paper on which was scribbled her destination.

"Then get your ass in the back and let's get going. The cars behind us aren't gonna wait much longer."

"Uh, I'm not quite sure how," Sela replied dubiously.

"Oh, for Chrissakes," the cabby complained. "Do all you women think I'm running some limo service?" Griping about the fact that certain television shows had, apparently, made his life a misery.

Opening the door, he gave Sela a facetious bow as she climbed in, shutting the door with a patronizing thunk.

Settling into his seat, he spotted the paper she had held, balanced on the edge of the front seat. Glancing into his mirror, he shook his head at his fare who was staring out of her window pensively.

As the taxi zipped along the streets, Sela, aware Peer would be suspicious of any redheads showing up, pondered whether she would be able to find anything suitable for what she had in mind.

The proprietor of the wig shop tried to convince Sela, she would look ravishing with blonde, flowing locks. Or better yet, with her cheekbones, she might even be able to pull off jet black with purple highlights.

Finally, Sela managed to get a word in edgewise, "Do you have anything in a mousy brown? Maybe shoulder length?"

The woman's sophisticated tone was betrayed by her Downtown upbringing, and she treated Sela to a skeptical eye. "Why in God's name would you want anything so hideous? You tryin' to ditch the cops or something?"

"If you don't want my business, I can find somebody..." Sela turned for the door.

"Hold your horses. Sheesh, I was just curious. Give me a few to check in the back. Don't get much call for something that ugly." The owner shrugged, heading to the storeroom.

Sela heard the woman's not so subtle mutterings about the crazy chick's stupid choice right up to when she reappeared. "Here you go, doll. If you don't want your boyfriend to know you're stalking him, this should do the trick." The clerk's snarky comment, as she pried further, made Sela laugh.

Sela satisfied her curiosity, "It's easier to hide from his wife this way."

The clerk nodded knowingly as she led Sela to a mirror on the counter where she tugged the wig into place and made sure it was secure.

After brushing it out, she stood back and said, "There ya go. Not even your own mother would recognize ya."

"You know, you're right." Sela turned her head from side to side, judging the reflection she saw.

"It's a good thing she is already dead, because if she saw me like this, it would probably kill her anyway."

The saleswoman had no witty comeback to this comment and, without appearing rude, ensured this peculiar customer departed her premises as quickly as possible.

Sela's second port of call was a sidewalk vendor's stall to purchase a pair of dark sunglasses and a hat.

As much as she missed the unspoiled beauty of her real home, there was something to be said about the variety of stuff you could buy with ease on any New York street.

Her third stop was a coffee shop within sight of Peer's house.

Sela sat in a window booth drinking coffee as she watched the army of caterers, trek in and out of the house like ants. Tables and chairs, buffet serving trays. It looked like Peer was pulling out all the stops. His vanity, as ever, had got the better of him.

Once the crew had disappeared into the house, Sela slipped out of the shop, and sauntered casually along her side of the street before crossing over to where the trucks were parked.

Secreting herself between the vehicles, she kept an ear peeled for anybody returning, while she sought what she needed.

In the last truck, she struck pay dirt, finding a neatly bound package. She added it to the other items in her bag and made good her getaway before anybody discovered her.

Pleased with her success, she set off for the subway, time to go home, and *maybe even tackle the mess I'm sure is still waiting for me.*

When she reached the entrance, she had a change of heart.

Checking to see whether Thomas had called — happy to note he had not — Sela turned off her phone and stuffed it into her coat.

If this was going to be her final day on Earth, she was not going to sacrifice it being herded by the priest.

Foregoing the subway, she walked towards Uptown, savoring every step she took as if it was her last.

The warmth of the sun made her feel alive and invigorated. Window shopping along the way made the time pass quickly as she headed for Central Park. It made perfect sense to spend whatever time there might be left where she first found herself.

Sitting in the shade of a huge tree, Sela let the sound of the park wash over her.

Children played under the watchful eyes of mothers or nannies. Some couples sat on the benches feeding the noisy pigeons, while others strolled hand-in-hand along the paths enjoying the early spring day.

The cheerful scene unfolding around her, left Sela feeling detached, alienated. She had long since acknowledged her mission meant more than ensuring she never *ever* returned to the rock, although she could not deny that was her primary personal motivation.

No, it had become a race to save these people who

wandered by her, oblivious to their pending extinction levied by a man, they had no clue existed.

If only they knew the barbarity Peer planned to wreak upon this world at the hands of Hel's army, if she, Sela, failed to destroy him.

Did any possess the fortitude of her own warriors to stand against him? Would anyone be willing to help her?

Sela was not naive. If she dared ask, she would find herself in a barred room, in that hospital Thomas had taken her to when he visited one of the parishioners, before finishing her petition.

Restlessly, she fidgeted on the bench, her sharp eye noting the curious conduct among those who passed each other in the park, perturbed by their determination to avoid any interaction.

Fair enough, they were probably strangers, but a quick 'Hello' or a smile never hurt anyone. A random act of kindness which might brighten an otherwise ordinary day.

The community in which she grew up, lived and died for one another. Here, in this so-called advanced era, it seemed no one cared for the well-being of their fellow man.

How life had changed. Sela's sympathy for these clueless mortals subsided marginally.

Maybe Peer was right? she philosophized. *Maybe they're not worth saving? They are as vacuous as the masses in Hell.* Sela had given up distinguishing between the different levels of Hell; much easier to encompass them all in one word.

A sudden twinge in her palm warned her the coin was probably about to make an unnecessary decision.

Dispelling that thought, she decided to spend what was left of the day amusing herself.

Previously, Sela's appreciation of New York was

confined to the darkness when it was silhouetted in the artificial glow of neon.

My first opportunity to view this city in all its glory, to delight and inveigle me. To demonstrate that my task is worthwhile.

Rising to her feet, she brushed herself off and left the park.

Purchasing a tourist map from one of the street vendors, Sela melded into the moving throng of people as they wound their way through the day.

She explored the museums, of which there seemed to be one on every corner. The antiquities, statuary, and artwork reminded her of the beauty, humanity had been creating since the dawn of time — even if, somewhere along the way, they had forgotten how to communicate with one another.

They also called to mind the innumerable and pointless wars, resulting in an egregious loss of life, all in pursuit of wealth. That brought her up with a jolt as she recalled her own greed and what that had set in motion. Perhaps the world hadn't changed after all.

In one museum, she joined a group being shepherded through the exhibits by an outwardly knowledgeable person. He took great pride in providing the minutest detail of some obscure battle or artist's brush stroke.

Until he steered the group to a display of Norse culture.

He embarked on a lecture declaring that the Vikings were a barbarous and superstitious lot, alleging their entire belief system was based on natural phenomena, used by those who wanted to gain mastery over gullible subjects and, what they believed to be magic was nothing more than herbal potions brewed by old crones.

The longer the guide flapped his lips, the more Sela wanted to find a dagger to slit his throat in the hope it would shut him up.

"My, but he does love to hear himself speak, doesn't he, my dear? Such an authority on the subject, most enjoyable."

Sela turned to see an elderly woman standing beside her. She had not heard anyone approach, but now found the woman's arm looped around hers.

Her face was ancient and worn, but her eyes shimmered a brilliant blue. Her smile warmed Sela, evoking her childhood when she whiled away hours talking with her grandmother.

"He has no right to insult a culture he has obviously only read about in some old musty book," Sela protested.

The woman patted Sela's arm and chuckled softly. "Never fear, my child, a thousand years from now, somebody just like him will be standing in front of another group and, with the same certitude, assert a completely different viewpoint.

"Always remember, while the names and faces of the gods may change, belief remains steadfast.

"Even those who say they believe in nothing still believe in themselves. Perhaps one day this blowhard will meet up with old Freya and find himself bound to a stone. *Then* we can discuss whether magic exists."

The old woman huffed in indignation at his arrogant assumption. "*Magic doesn't exist...* the gall."

Amused and surprised, Sela was about to agree with the

elderly lady, but she was nowhere to be seen; vanishing as quickly as she had appeared.

Sela's grin, provoked by the woman's chagrin, broadened as she finished the tour and returned to the sunny street.

Suffering from a surfeit of museums and the past, Sela spent the rest of the day in the present, meandering the streets; enjoying being part of the hustle and bustle that was quintessentially New York and, in the same spirit, stopped at a small deli for a bite to eat.

She had grown to love the international tastes of this city.

Occasionally, she missed the delicacies of her own time and home, but found, like so many others before her, that she had a weakness for a really fine pizza. If this was going to be her last meal, why not?

She ordered a deluxe Chicago-style with every topping she could think of. The guy behind the counter gaped at her as he listened to her order.

Shaking his head in disbelief at her appetite, he clipped the order to the stainless-steel order rack sitting in the window which separated him from the cook, and spun it to his coworker, bursting into laughter when the slip of a girl ordered a diet drink to go with her meal.

Settling into one of the chairs set by a table outside of the cafe, Sela savored her pizza as the city passed her by.

She had one stop left before she returned home and wanted to get there before the sun set.

Tucking the last few slices into a carryout box, she left.

The sidewalks had thinned as the afternoon waned, making her trek easier.

She encountered a homeless man with a mangy dog, begging on one of the corners. Without a second thought, she handed him her pizza and wished him a good life.

The beggar grunted something about preferring cash but tore into the pizza, tossing a wedge to his dog.

It wasn't until Sela reached her final destination that she behaved like a typical tourist and looked up.

Above her, towered the Empire State Building. It was indeed impressive and seemed to ascend for miles. She hurried inside to take the elevator to the Observation Deck on the 102nd floor.

The sun was beginning to set as she reached the deck and she was held in thrall as the golden rays cooled to magnificent splashes of orange and red, before dying into deep hues of violet and black.

Because the city was never totally dark, only the brightest of stars made their presence known.

Those stars represented Sela's family.

Even if New York would never know what she did for it, those stars would. She would. She was not about to lose to Peer.

Not this time, nor ever again.

Happy with her day, it was time to go home. Before she got into the elevator, she turned her phone on. It immediately began its ceaseless chime of missed calls from the priest.

Sela smiled and called him back.

"Thomas, I'll be home in about an hour, by which time, I expect a clean kitchen and dinner on the table."

THIRTEEN

Despite his cool façade, Peer was anxious when the doorbell rang. He knew who was coming and had planned exactly how he was going to rid himself of the cursed bitch once and for all.

His eyes overshot the idiot priest's shoulder when he opened the door, welcoming them to his party with artificial sincerity — more interested in the woman accompanying the God botherer.

With all the tuxedos and gowns crammed into the house, the drab habit of the nun stuck out like a sore thumb. The woman refused to lift her head while the two men continued their absurd platitudes, joking about fleecing the flock for a good cause.

Peer wanted her to look up at him, wanted to see the terror in her eyes when she recognized him and accepted her fate, but she waited passively and, to Peer's aggravation, appeared to be... ***bored***.

Thomas shifted his stance in order to introduce the nun.

"May I introduce Sister Mary Catherine, Mother Superior at the Sisters of the Forlorn Souls? She runs the house where women who have been lured into life on the street can find assistance, and will also be the recipient of any donations we receive this evening."

Peer extended his hand, determined to end this charade right here, but when the woman accepted the formality of the handshake, she lifted her face. To his chagrin, she was not Sela. She was an aged nun with an incredibly firm grasp.

Have I read the priest wrong? Has this comfortable life blurred my judgement? No, I cannot be mistaken. Peer's certainty this man was nothing more than a puppet in Sela's game, overrode his reservations.

The idea Thomas might be exactly what he said he was — a priest looking for actual donations, was confounding.

Peer gawked at the nun, until he felt her hand slip through his arm.

"Shall we meet your generous guests and see whether they might be willing to help those in need?" The nun steered Peer towards the waiting ensemble.

Peer glanced back to see Thomas smile and shrug as the woman led him away.

He managed a muttered, "It would be my pleasure."

Following the pair, Thomas listened to Sister Mary explain about the desperate situation the House had found itself in, and how fortunate they were to have such a charitable benefactor.

Thomas laughed inwardly at the nun's saccharin-sweet sales pitch, sure she would keep Peer occupied for much of the evening.

It gave him time to attend to more important matters.

At his most urbane, Thomas mingled with the assemblage of rich, old men — who had, clearly and not necessarily successfully, employed every weapon at their disposal to tap the fountain of youth — and their skimpily clad, overly-perfumed, trophy wives.

He used them as a cover to circle the room and make small talk, creating the impression he was involved in several conversations.

With a sigh of relief, he reached the door, only to have his progress arrested by a bland voice asking a question.

"Would you care for some hors d'oeuvres, Father?"

He turned to see a waitress with mousy brown hair, presenting a platter of goose liver pâté. His brow quirked when he spotted the slight wrinkle of her nose at the smell of the paste.

In undertones, she said, "I will never understand how you people can eat this crap."

"It's an acquired taste. Personally, I'm more of a canned Spam guy. Did you have any trouble getting in?"

"That's even more disgusting, and no, the caterer was too busy tossing trays at his wait staff to notice an extra set of hands.

"Speaking of which, may I hand this off to you, kind sir? I have a crime to serve up," Sela's words were augmented by her most persuasive smile as she tried to divert Thomas and rid herself of the disgusting canapés in one swift motion.

"Oh, no you don't," Thomas objected, refusing the platter. "I'm coming with you."

"We've been through this already, Thomas." Surreptitiously, Sela surveyed the crowd to make sure no one was paying attention to a priest flirting with a waitress.

"I need you here to make sure our host stays put. It should only take me a couple of minutes to retrieve the blades and get the hell out of here. If I need your help, I'll call your phone. Now, if you'll excuse me..." She left Thomas staring after her as she vanished through the door, the tray still in hand.

The sounds of the party receded to muffled din as Sela made her way towards the staircase Thomas had indicated, taking care to avoid being noticed.

She elected to keep the heavy tray with her to maintain her disguise as one of the wait staff wandering the house serving the guests.

Under the circumstances, Sela assumed Peer would have a security detachment patrolling the residence not only to protect the walking money in the main hall, but also his cherished collection on the upper floor.

To her surprise, she found a single guard positioned at the foot of the stairs.

Approaching with breezy confidence, she observed him slide his hand unobtrusively to cover the grip of his holstered pistol.

"Where do you think you're going, missy?" the guard challenged.

"I was instructed to bring this cat puke up to Mr. Bjorg's game room because he wants to show off his toys to a bunch of his bigwigs," Sela countered in an, 'I really couldn't give a toss' tone.

"Nobody told me about it," the guard's voice was tinged with irritation. He hated working for these self-entitled rich people who would change arrangements on a whim, without informing security.

"Until I hear differently, **nobody** goes upstairs."

Sela shrugged, "Hey, that's ok with me. This tray weighs a ton and I didn't want to lug it up all those stairs, anyway.

"If I were you, though, I'd get on your little radio and

check with whomever. It's not my ass in a sling when his guests starve to death because they couldn't gorge themselves on these tasty dog treats."

The guard hesitated, *should he call or send this bitch packing*. Resolving to let a higher pay grade make that decision, he relaxed his grip on his pistol, and twiddled with the transmit button on his two-way.

That was all Sela needed.

Before the guard, literally and figuratively, knew what had hit him, Sela cold-cocked him with the tray.

The thud was louder than she intended, but it had served its purpose, as the guard crumpled in an untidy heap on the bottom stair.

In two minds as to whether he might be considered an innocent, she took a second to check she had not killed him.

Satisfied he would wake up, eventually, she lugged his limp body into one of the rooms further down the hall.

"Sleep well, and I'm sorry for the headache you're gonna have when you come to," Sela said facetiously as she flicked the lock then closed the door with a quiet *click*.

Returning to the scene of the crime, she scooped up the splattered pâté as best as she could.

Dropping the remnants on the dented platter, Sela raced up the stairs before anybody else thought to stop her.

At the top, she found herself faced with the heavy doors Thomas had warned her about.

Kneeling, Sela examined the lock. Its bizarre design and construction, obviously something Peer had concocted with his magic.

Retrieving her little kit, Sela endeavored to pick the

lock, but try as she might, she could not make the tumblers fall into place.

She rocked back on her heels. Evidently, it required a particular key and nothing else would disengage the mechanism.

She pounded the door with her fist, fighting angry tears. *To come this far and be thwarted at the final hurdle is beyond frustrating.*

"Your magic exists, little one. Just believe."

Sela swung around to see who had snuck up on her, but the landing was empty. She grumbled balefully, "My whole world is about to fall apart and now I'm hearing voices as well. Isn't that just awesome?"

"Less of the dramatics. If you're going to give up that easily, you deserve what's about to happen to you."

Sela recognized the voice as that of the woman from the museum, but couldn't figure out how...

A sharp pain in her palm forced her to look at her hand. The hideous gnarled face of the coin gleamed with a golden light she had never seen before.

The pain it caused was excruciating and prevented her from closing her hand.

"Turn the damned knob **now**, little one. Have faith in your own magic."

Sela's eyes brimmed with tears as she faced the door. Involuntarily, she reached for the doorknob, unable to control the movement. The glow engulfed the handle which shattered under her touch.

Dumbfounded, she watched the great door swing open on its hinges, soundlessly.

A quick glance at her hand revealed nothing except the ugly scar. Simultaneously swearing and thanking her invisible accomplice, Sela, exercising extreme caution, stepped inside.

Entering Peer's trophy room, blackness swamped her, sending an eerie chill of recognition down her spine. Sela was positive she had returned to where this whole execrable tale began.

She tried to retreat, to escape, but a flicker from beyond one of the cases caught her eye, halting her flight. Gradually, the flicker transformed into an apparition. Convinced, Peer was trying to catch her unarmed, Sela readied herself for his attack.

The face which emerged from the light was not the viscously handsome countenance she had grown to despise.

No, the features of the apparition were, at first, ancient beyond description, then suddenly young and beautiful.

It was the Goddess, Freya.

Sela gaped slack jawed as the shimmering image manifested.

"I get you into this room, and you prefer to stand there gawking, girl?" Freya sounded more disappointed than she had in the hallway.

"Odin's... no... my goddess. *You* are responsible for all of this? I thought it was..."

"Loki?" Freya spat the name.

The paradoxical nature of her relationship with the Trickster God was legendary and Sela knew better than to interrupt.

"No one knows what that worthless pile of dung is up to. I am here because I am weary of the pissing contest between Peer and him for Helheim, and to use you as a pawn is inexcusable."

Astonished, Sela blurted out, "You are here to help me fight? I'm not worthy of such an honor…"

"No, my child you most certainly are not," Freya was quick to assure. "I am well aware you remain accountable for what you did when a queen, and to rectify *this* mess, is your responsibility. My presence is solely to ensure a level playing field."

Freya studied the exhibit in front of her, and as Sela's gaze followed, it dawned on her where they stood.

Her blades.

Under the iridescence radiating from Freya, they appeared bathed in fire.

Sela assumed the goddess would reach through the repository to retrieve the swords, but Freya opted for a less subtle route.

"I'd shield your eyes if I were you," Freya cautioned.

Before Sela could open her mouth to ask why, Freya had destroyed the case in one fell swoop.

Pulverized glass shards tumbled like ice chips to the wooden floor. Sela's twin swords were free at last.

Abruptly, the room was flooded with light.

"If I judge Peer's useless magic correctly, I recommend you do not waste time admiring your shiny trinkets," Freya warned, plucking the weapons from the wreckage of the display case.

"It looks like you are about to meet his personal guards."

The instant the case disintegrated, tortured wails began to emanate from the periphery of the room, amplifying by the second.

The first of the figures, Peer had draped in armor, drew breath.

Turning to Freya, Sela grasped the swords. Her hands had not wrapped around these glorious hilts in centuries, but it felt no longer than a day.

Testing her swing, Sela felt Freya touch her wrists. An enhanced strength and agility, hitherto unknown, flowed through her body.

"Do not lose, Sela," was all Freya instructed, transforming Sela into a Berserker warrior, and unleashing the slender hellion of fury upon the advancing horde of Peer's undead.

FOURTEEN

Sela brandished her blades wildly in all directions as the guard closed in on her.

Instinct, ingrained for millennia, came to the fore and her haphazard flailing became brutally methodical as she hacked through the mass.

The sound of bone shattering reverberated around the room. Sela's decimation was accentuated by the demonic screams as she tore through them.

The glint of steel sparkled in the glare of the spotlights.

Each blade severing her attackers' heads.

Sela yelped when the bite of an aged sword lacerated her side. She swung about, ramming her own blade deep into the eye socket of the owner of the lucky strike.

Corkscrewing her weapon back and forth, Sela ripped it out of the empty cavity, tearing apart the demon's face.

Drenched in black blood, her breathing as jagged and as frenzied as her assault, she refused to cede, vowing to fight to the last.

As quickly as the battle had commenced, the legions

vanished, leaving nothing save the discarded, empty armor strewn about the floor.

The fury consuming Sela subsided, and she reoriented herself.

Freya had gone and, with her, any of the guards who had not found liberation at the end of Sela's blades.

The strange incandescence which had illuminated the trophy room, dimmed.

A shaft of light from the hall cleaved a path into the room, silhouetting two figures, the second of whom was slightly behind the first.

The pair stopped short of where Sela waited.

She lowered her blades to her side when she saw Peer using Thomas as a shield.

While her relaxed stance might have fooled those who did not know her, she was poised to dissect Peer to his death.

In the same way she had dispatched his spectral guards, she would dispense with him.

Irritation flickered across her face as the two advanced into the room. Peer's fingers were digging into the sensitive skin at the crook of Thomas's neck, and Sela presumed the tip of his blade was pressed to Thomas's back.

"Let the priest go, you coward. He has nothing to do with this fight," Sela demanded. "This is between us."

"Then maybe I should kill him now for helping you make such a mess in here. After all, isn't sacrifice part of his calling?" Peer mocked as he increased his pressure.

The tip of the blade punctured Thomas's flesh causing him to wince.

"***Stop it, Peer***," Sela screamed.

"Well now, my pretty, we have come full circle. You

reclaimed what you had so carelessly discarded — your freedom — and left me with nothing in return."

Tutting, Peer shook Thomas. "Bad form Sela, bad form. Fear not, I am about to rectify your oversight by relieving you of something you appear to cherish more than that stupid coin.

"The only difference, bitch, is that when *I'm* done, I shall return home in triumph and you will suffer for eternity with even greater anguish knowing you cost the life of this *innocent*."

Sela paused and looked Thomas dead in the eye.

The all too familiar jolt of pain shot through the palm of her hand as the cursed coin readied itself for the question, but she already had the answer.

She beamed disarmingly. "Go on then."

"Did you hear what I said, woman? I'm going to kill your priest. Don't think I won't," a hint of confusion laced Peer's threat.

Floored, Thomas studied Sela, unable to credit she was willing to toss a man's life away like yesterday's dinner.

Sela did not waver.

"I heard you, Peer," she raised her blade. "Do it or release him. Right now, he's just in the way."

With a careless shrug, Peer plunged his knife into Thomas's back, burying the blade to the hilt.

Peer shoved the dying man forwards in an attempt to knock Sela off balance and retrieve his blade in one swift motion.

Things don't always go as planned.

Thomas's body seemed to clench about the blade and refused to relinquish it, tearing the knife out of Peer's grasp.

Unarmed, momentum carried Peer and the dead priest

into Sela. As she stepped backwards to avoid them, Peer lunged, knocking one of her swords from her grip.

Before Sela could recover, Peer had leaped to his feet to face her, wielding the blade.

She sliced the air a couple of times with the remaining one, readying herself.

The adversaries circled each other.

Peer jabbed at Sela in an attempt to draw her in, but Sela knew better than to attack until the opportune moment. When she did not bite, he swung the blade in earnest.

Sela blocked the wild thrust easily, sparks from the swords clashing, split the darkness. The clang of metal on metal resounded as the fight intensified.

Even though Sela had learned her skill from Peer, she acknowledged he was the superior warrior, her dexterity dulled by lack of practice, and being bound to a rock in Niflheim hadn't helped.

No fool, Peer played with her, treating this as nothing more deadly than a game of chess with him one move ahead. Like a Grandmaster, he used every trick in the book to unsettle Sela. He feinted, obliging her to parry to the left until she was at her most vulnerable, then swerved to nick her right ear.

"Come now, Sela, your pathetic defense brings shame on me as your teacher," Peer taunted, striking her temple. "Concede so I don't have to carve up that beautiful body of yours."

When he attempted to repeat the humiliating attack a fourth time, Sela anticipated the move and, as Peer's blade arced to notch her uninjured ear, she upended the hilt to counter the blow.

"Finally," Peer smirked. "For a moment there, I thought proceedings ought to be delayed so I could retrain you."

"Fuck you," was Sela's succinct riposte.

The longer the duel lasted, the more proficient Sela became; her muscle memory and natural expertise manifesting with extraordinary celerity.

At one with the blade, Sela's advance was uncompromising, her deflections effortless.

Peer was endlessly relieved that, despite the hours spent training Sela, he still had a few dirty tricks up his sleeve, aware, if he didn't take the upper hand soon, it would be too late.

Their blades locked together. Peer seized his chance and jabbed his elbow into her neck, propelling her into a display case, spluttering for air and clutching her throat.

The impact sent Sela and the cabinet toppling to the ground in an explosion of glass.

Peer slashed at her chest, the tip of his blade piercing her back as she rolled away.

Howling in pain, and heedless of the damage she was inflicting on herself, Sela netted a handful of slivers and flung them at Peer's face.

His focus shifted, giving Sela the opening, she needed.

As Peer tried to avoid the hail of splinters, Sela, half-upright, rammed into his gut, grabbing him around his waist, and driving him to the floor.

Peer pounded her shoulders with the pommel of his sword, but their joint impetus was too great and he teetered, landing flat on his back.

The blind fury of Freya's champion returned with a vengeance. Sela straddled Peers' chest, pummeling his face with the hilt of her blade.

Peer had drilled into her that it was not enough to kill her opponent in hand-to-hand combat, she needed to destroy them.

A lesson, Sela was about to execute with relish.

He labored to dislodge her but, inexplicably, failed. *Was Freya's magic pinning him in place?*

Whatever it was, Sela used it to her advantage, battering his skull like a piñata. Blood spilled from Peer's inky eyes, trickled out of his ears, and gushed from his nose with her relentless strikes.

Peer pleaded with her to spare his life, once again promising undreamed of power and prestige, if only she would yield.

Sela had other ideas.

Satisfied he was unable to defend himself, she relieved his hand of her other sword and crossed them, scissor-like under his chin.

"I think your skull will make a nice decorative planter, you viperous, puke-stockinged turd."

With a singularly sweet smile, Sela braced herself, and jerked the blades together with savage emphasis. She was unable to prevent a sardonic chuckle when, recognizing his demise was inescapable, Peer's eyes bulged in horrified disbelief.

Too late.

Blood erupted from his throat, spraying the ceiling in a neat arc as his head was sheared from his body.

Casually, Sela wiped the gore coating her beloved swords on his expensive tux.

Rising to her feet, she padded across the floor, nudging Thomas's body with her foot as she passed, in search of a set of scabbards to sheathe her blades.

"You would make a more plausible corpse if you were actually bleeding, Thom... or do you prefer Loki?" she lectured breezily.

"*You let him stab me,*" the cadaver complained crossly from its huddled position.

"Get your whiny butt up, or *I'll* stab you. Bearing in mind you've concealed your identity from me all this time, I should do it anyway. Odin knows you deserve it.

"You were in the way. Had Peer not done the deed, you would have felt the sting of my blade. While neither option was particularly desirable — from your perspective — I do believe the latter was guaranteed to piss you off more," Sela tutted and, tired of talking to Loki's backside, hauled him to his feet.

"How did you know you were right?" Loki shot back, irascibly. "What if your little gamble had failed and he *had* killed me?"

"I guess Freya would be showering me in praise, and I'd have to contend with your daughter.

"As for gambling with your life, *you* set the rules." Sela brushed the dust off Thomas's... Loki's... tunic.

"Obviously it didn't matter to Peer one way or the other. So, if an innocent was killed, as long as I didn't wield the death blow, you were safe," she paused before adding, "Then again, how innocent *are* you in the first place?"

Loki arched a brow, contemplating admonishing her for such insolence, but she was right and he knew it. *What was the old adage? Discretion is the better part of valor.*

He buttoned his lip.

"Why didn't *you* take care of Peer?" Hands on hips, Sela narrowed her gaze. "You are a god after all. Why make me do it?"

"Because you created him. It was your magic which gave him his strength, and your anger fed him. Besides, where was the fun in me doing it?"

"You are incorrigible. No wonder most of Valhalla wants your head." Sela rolled her eyes expressively, and wagged a tolerant finger, saying gravely, "What happens now?"

"That's totally up to you, Sela Helsdatter. You're at liberty to walk away and live out your life here on Earth, after which you may be granted entry into Odin's hallowed halls, or..."

"*Or*?" Sela was curious, yet somehow aware of what he was going to ask. She wanted to hear him say it.

"Stay with me. In my entire existence, there has been only one other about whom I cared, and that was half-hearted at best.

"Then I met you.

"Without trying, you have become more important to me than breathing, as recent events attest..." his wink was nothing short of wicked, "...and, if you say no, I shall be reduced to stalking you, which I reckon is too dangerous, even for me."

"First, it's called being in love, you idiot. Second, I hate the last name you gave me."

"Really? Hel thought it was cute."

"Of course, she did, which merely reinforces my point."

Loki knew she was right.

Still, being Loki, he could not help but tease, "Never mind, given the way bureaucracy runs in Helheim, it will probably take a few millennia to change your last name. I'm sure you'll grow to love me way before then."

Which earned him a small fist to his gut.

"Anymore cracks like that, mister, and you had best learn to love that response. As for your question..." Sela looked at the scar in her palm.

"Really? You are willing to let that hideous coin decide the rest of your life?"

"No, but if you don't get your butt over here and kiss me, I *will* ask it whether *not* killing you was the right choice."

Loki needed no further invitation and pulled the flame-haired, if rather bloodied, beauty into his arms.

Sela's eyes drifted closed and a delicious frisson rippled down her spine in anticipation of the kiss she would have died for.

It didn't happen, and she was startled when the tingle she expected to feel on her lips came from her palm.

Opening her eyes, Sela saw Loki flipping a coin.

The one which had scarred not only her hand but also her very soul.

He gave a roguish grin. "We have to pay for the cab ride home somehow."

Their soft laughter, the first step in erasing the nightmare Peer had wrought.

As though they had all the time in the world, Loki curved a hand around Sela's cheek, and gazed into her incredible eyes, conveying his heart's desire in a tacit but unequivocal message.

What he read in the brilliant blue depths, elicited a sigh which echoed across millennia and, gently, he molded her to his muscular frame.

Long suppressed and once forgotten emotions,

coalesced into a passionate kiss which went on and on and on, full of life, and love, and promises of forever.

Free at last, Sela was in control of her own destiny and, she surmised, of Loki's for good measure.

Unadulterated joy suffused her whole being... her fate no longer bound to a flip of the coin.

CONCEIVED CHAOS SYNOPSIS
THE SELA HELSDATTER SAGA

Book Two

After ridding the world of her tormenter, and finding the love of her life, Sela Helsdatter could be forgiven for thinking she deserves a little peace.

No such luck!

Marriage to the God of Mischief is a walk in the park compared with the terror about to be unleashed from Valhalla. A diabolical edict from Odin himself sees the nine months pregnant, Sela fleeing from the entire Norse pantheon, with no clue why.

A price on her head and a target on her belly, the only person she can trust is her husband, who is keeping her in the dark.

Does her unborn child hold the key to this Conceived Chaos?

About the Author
RORI BLEU

With a smattering of riverboat pirates and royalty in her heritage, Rori Bleu's childhood reflected her past.
An interest in fairy tales, myth and legend were as important as spirited discussions around politics and current affairs — although some might argue they are one and the same!

A fascination, sparked by listening to Grimm's Fairy Tales at her grandmother's knee, not only encouraged Rori's passion for reading, but also steered her into the world of RPG's.
What began as a fun pastime, soon evolved into the creation of fantastical worlds, but Rori never lost her love of politics going on to specialise in Governmental History and Historical Research.

Naturally this means her stories are steeped in historical accuracy and real-life intrigue. While Rori's love of a happily ever after means her preferred genre is romance, don't be surprised if you discover an occasional detour into historical fiction, thrillers, horror and fantasy.

To find more of Rori's books... click the link
https://linktr.ee/roribleu

About the Author

ABOUT THE AUTHOR
ROSIE CHAPEL

Rosie Chapel lives in Perth, Australia with her hubby and two furkids. When not writing, she loves catching up with friends, burying herself in a book (or three), discovering the wonders of Western Australia, or — and the best — a quiet evening at home with her husband, enjoying a glass of wine and a movie.

Website: www.rosiechapel.com

ALSO BY RORI BLEU

Pineapple Meringue

Imprisoned Hearts

Port of London

Dani's Masquerade

Black Tulips

Ajei's Destiny

Porta Aeternum

The Queen's Heart

Syn *with Matthew Forester*

Echoes and Illusions *with Rosie Chapel*

Evie's War *with Rosie Chapel*

Vindicta *with Rosie Chapel*

ALSO BY ROSIE CHAPEL

<u>Historical Fiction</u>

The Hannah's Heirloom Sequence

The Pomegranate Tree - Book One

Echoes of Stone and Fire - Book Two

Embers of Destiny - Book Three

Etched in Starlight - Prequel

Hannah's Heirloom Trilogy - Compilation — e-book only

Prelude to Fate

Legacy of Flame and Ash

The Nettleby Trilogy (WW1 Novellas)

A Guardian Unexpected- Book One

Under the Clock - Book Two

Evie's War *with Rori Bleu*

Vindicta *with Rori Bleu*

<u>Regency Romances</u>

The Linen and Lace Series

Once Upon An Earl - Book One

To Unlock Her Heart - Book Two

Love on a Winter's Tide - Book Three

A Love Unquenchable - Book Four

A Hidden Rose — Book Five

The Daffodil Garden

The Unconventional Duchess

Rescuing Her Knight - *the de Wiltons:* Book One

Elusive Hearts - *An Unexpected Romance*: Book One

His Fiery Hoyden

A Regency Duet

A Regency Christmas Double

Fate is Curious

A Christmas Prayer *with Ashlee Shades*

The Lady's Wager

Winning Emma

A Love Impossible

Unravelling Roana

Love Kindled

Moonbeams and Mistletoe

<u>Fairy Tale Romance</u>

Chasing Bluebells

<u>Contemporary Romances</u>

Of Ruins and Romance

All At Once It's You

Cobweb Dreams

Just One Step

His Heart's Second Sigh

<u>Dystopian Romance</u>

Echoes & Illusions *with Rori Bleu*